HANG TOWN

Also by Lee Martin

Shadow on the Mesa
Fast Ride to Boot Hill
The Last Wild Ride
The Grant Conspiracy: Wake of the Civil War
Fury at Cross Creek
In Mysterious Ways
Revenge at Rawhide
The Maverick Gun
Fury at Sweetwater Pass
The Lone Rider
Black River
Dead Man's Trail
Valley of the Lawless
Track the Men Down
The Danger Trail

The Darringer Brothers Series:

Trail of the Fast Gun
Trail of the Long Riders
Trail of the Hunter
Trail of the Circle Star
Trail of the Restless Gun
Trail of the Dangerous Gun

and coming soon…

The Siege at Rhyker's Station

HANG TOWN

LEE MARTIN

VACA MOUNTAIN PRESS
VACAVILLE, CALIFORNIA, USA

Vaca Mountain Press
Paperback ISBN 13: 978-1-952380-47-1
Kindle ISBN 13: 978-1-952380-48-8

Also available in
Large Print ISBN 13: 978-1-952380-49-5

Cover design by Christopher Wait, ENC Graphic Services
Cover images © Getty Images
Interior design by Deirdre Wait, ENC Graphic Services

Published by Vaca Mountain Press

Visit Lee Martin Westerns on Facebook.

To all of my wonderful family,
and in the fond memory of
my beloved mother,
my beautiful sister Arlene,
our rough riding brothers,
and for Jim Liontas.

HANG TOWN

ONE

On a miserable night in the spring of 1869, not far from Denver City in Colorado Territory, a small boy of twelve headed for home on his old bay gelding. Wind and rain spun off his hat brim and whistled down his yellow slicker. Named Joey, the boy's thoughts reflected the grim set of his mouth and the brimming tears in his ice-blue eyes.

"He sticks my head in the trough again, I'm gonna run away."

Between being angry and wanting to cry, Joey felt tortured and helpless.

All around him, aspens swayed in the dark storm like monsters with shaggy arms. Lodgepole pines stood strong and tall but spooky with their long needles shaking in the rising wind. His horse jumped when a critter darted nearby. Yet Joey preferred the scary storm and dangers of the night to what lay ahead. Small for his age, he always tried to stand taller than he was, but it wasn't enough to save him.

* * *

As he rode through the trees toward the horse barn on the Lassiter spread, he saw lamplight behind the shutters in the single level ranch house to his left. Outside the garden gate, the doctor's gray buggy horse stood with its head down in the rain.

Knowing of his mother's poor health, Joey was grateful the doctor always came when called. Unable to protect her or himself, he wavered between wanting to be near and his readiness to take flight.

Under his slicker and worn clothes, he felt his skin prickle with the ever increasing chill. Any moment, he thought he would turn into an icicle. His feet numb in his boots, he worried he wouldn't be able to stand up once he dismounted.

Far back from the house and barn, the bunk house had a light in the window and smoke coming from the chimney, fighting the rain. More lights gleamed from the cook house near it. Every flickering glimmer seemed eerie in the storm.

Beyond the ranch buildings and trees, cattle fended for themselves on the range.

Joey worried when he saw the light of a lamp burning just inside the horse barn.

He made a face as he thought, *Pa better not be in there.*

With no choice, he rode inside through the wide open barn door, where other horses stood in the far stalls. Not seeing anyone, he hoped the lamp had been left burning by accident. Weary, cold and dripping wet, he slid from the saddle near the empty stall he would use.

He removed his hat with the red embroidered band to shake off the rain and smooth his dark brown hair before replacing it. He loosened the red wool scarf tucked under his leather coat and slicker. Both the scarf and hat band had been his mother's handiwork before she became ill, so he treasured them.

Shaking from exhaustion, prickly chills and mounting fear, he readied to unsaddle his horse when he would have preferred to escape to the unknown. Anywhere away from here. Held only by his concern for his frail mother, he steeled himself for another miserable night.

Pausing all of a sudden, he spotted a gunny sack on the straw in the empty stall, and he knew something was wrong. He looked inside to see his belongings, clothes, and a round of bread.

A loud, gruff voice close behind him caused him to spin.

"About time you got home."

A heavy hand whacked Joey in the jaw, sending him flying backwards and down onto the straw where he rolled against the side of the empty stall. Nearby, his horse threw up its head and backed away.

Joey gasped in pain. He fought the same old terror as he looked up at his father.

Harry Joseph Lassiter, a husky, thirty-eight-year-old man with a thin black mustache, hovered like a giant in the pale light of the lamp, throwing his shadow over Joey. Big and powerful, his hat pushed back from black hair shining with grease, he wore his all-too-deadly sidearm under his black coat. His pale gray eyes flashed with hatred.

Lassiter snarled. "I know you been skipping school, and I don't care why or where you been, because I want you out of here. Tonight."

Joey struggled to his feet, hanging on to the stall's side. Sick to his stomach from the blow, he could barely stand upright. He had never felt so small and helpless in front of this big man before, who continued to berate him all the more.

"Your ma just lost another kid, and it's your fault. She keeps trying because she don't want you no more."

Joey, having heard that over and over, had come to believe it. He was tired of being battered, always where the bruises would not show. Except tonight with a blow to his jaw. This new, brazen act terrified him. He feared his father was about to kill him, maybe bury him where he could not be found.

Lassiter held his hand on his holster. "Hit the road. Now!"

Joey hunched over, head spinning, jaw feeling cracked. He fought for breath. His skin crawled with fear. His vision blurred as he inhaled dust from the crackling straw.

"You get on that old nag of yours and get," Lassiter said to the boy. "Don't you tell nobody or I'll have to shut 'em up for good. Don't you write any letters or I'll hunt you down. And don't you ever come back, or I'll drown you in that trough."

Joey could barely stand. He knew every word would come true if he fought back.

Lassiter stormed out of the barn, into the rain, and headed for the house.

Joey wiped at his burning eyes, finally able to see straight.

Unaware of why his father hated him so much, Joey knew only one thing—he had to get away. He calmed his horse, took up his bag of clothes and tied it behind the pommel. He took a canteen from the wall, shook it to find it nearly full, and hooked it over the horn.

Peering out to be sure his father had gone in the house, Joey then dug into the grain box for the leather pouch full of coins he had earned. Skipping school to work at the rail yard whenever he could, he had been sweeping out warehouses where he could not be seen by anyone who would tell his father. He had saved every cent.

"Lord," he prayed, "'help me get away. Help me find my way."

Maybe the lights from the town would help guide him east to the rail yard. His horse knew the road. With heavy rain beating loudly on the barn roof, he prayed he would not get lost.

But all the while, his anger was focused on his father. "Someday I'm gonna be bigger than you, and I'll have a six shooter that's so fast, you'll run away crying like a scared rabbit."

Once mounted, he pulled his hat down tight and headed back the way he had come. The storm continued to blow, windy, wet and dark.

Inside the Lassiter house, the elderly doctor stood at Leslie Lassiter's bedside, alone with her in the bedroom where ivory lace curtains hung over white window shades. The only light came through the open door. Adjusting his spectacles, he talked softly. Already feeling the sedative, her eyes closed and she barely heard his voice.

"Are you in pain?"

Leslie, thirty years old and frail, shook her head, already beyond reason. Her soft brown hair lay damp about her pretty face. Heavy quilts seemed to have stopped her shivering. Limp and exhausted, she drifted into a deep sleep.

The doctor left her, closing the door behind him as he entered the well-kept front room where a fire crackled red and white in the hearth and lamps burned brightly. He gathered his supplies under the watchful gaze of the aging, very grim housekeeper Mrs. Katz. The white haired, dumpy woman forced a smile, her clothes drab under a smeared gray apron.

"She's asleep," he told the woman.

Abruptly, Lassiter, shed of his wet coat, entered the front room with hat in hand as Mrs. Katz went back to the kitchen. He peered carefully into the bedroom, allowing light to enter and seeing Leslie in deep slumber.

Lassiter closed the door on sight of her and turned to the doctor, who closed his bag and took up his long black coat.

"I gave her something to sleep," the doctor said as he donned his coat and a floppy brimmed hat. "The bleeding has stopped, but she needs to stay in bed another week."

"All right," Lassiter said, " at least she's still young enough to try again. She made it much longer this time."

Having warned him about the dangers many times, the doctor did not respond. He knew better than to argue with a man like Lassiter. He left without another word.

With the doctor gone and Mrs. Katz in the kitchen, Lassiter reentered the bedroom, leaving the door open again for the light. He stared down at his wife, so beautiful and dear to him. She had just turned thirty and had suffered her third miscarriage. Asleep with the drug, she didn't move.

Lassiter sat on the edge of the bed and stroked her hand, for he loved her more than a man should love a woman, so intense and so possessive. Yet he wanted another child—a son—no matter what.

"You sleep now, Leslie, and when you're up and around, we'll go buy you some new pretties," he said, "and don't you worry about Joey. He understands, and he really wants a little brother, so we just won't give up, will we?"

* * *

Later that same rainy night, Joey rode south, bent over in the cold rain, retracing his steps and turning left at the last pine to where he thought lay the road. To his right, he could see the lights scattered in the town of Denver—which now had nearly 5,000 people and was growing fast, as it continued to rebuild after a devastating fire. Stacks of bricks, along with tarp-covered lumber, lined some streets, with water swirling about.

Trusting his mount to stay on the trail heading east, Joey kept praying they would find their way through the storm.

Suddenly, the rain turned to drizzle on a rising wind from the north, and then no further rain fell from the sky.

Up in the dark heavens, a half moon flickered behind passing clouds, and then appeared, guiding him with a steady light.

Joey whispered his thanks while praying the moon stayed with him.

He rode far east of town and into the poorly-lit rail yard. No one was in sight. Box cars and flat beds sat on the rails. One engine could be seen in the pale light of the moon. The rain had stopped with an aggressive north wind.

A few protected lanterns burned on shacks near the platforms.

Beyond and central, a sign on a building proclaimed: **Denver Pacific Railway**. Here, unknown to his parents or any of the ranch hands, he had been secretly working after—and sometimes during—school.

He dismounted in front of a shack with lamplight at the rain smeared window. The sign by the door read: Guard Shack. He tied the reins to a post, then staggered over and banged on the door. Shaking with a chill and painful jaw, Joey had to draw on every ounce of strength he had.

After a moment, the door opened.

Staring at the boy, Higgins—an average-sized, clean-shaven man of fifty-eight with dark brown eyes and thinning hair, wearing dark denim clothes—quickly led him inside and closed the door against the cold night. With a pronounced limp favoring his right leg, Higgins moved to shepherd Joey to the warmth of the stove where a stew pot steamed and smelled of hot spices.

"My God, Joey, your face is all red."

The shack was cluttered with stacks of newspapers collected from all over, along with a few dime novels. Rifles hung on the wall. A gray cap reading "Rail Guard" hung next to them.

Higgins helped the boy remove his slicker.

Joey shook off his hat and sank on a chair as he warmed his hands by the iron stove. "My pa told me to get."

"What?"

Suddenly free to unburden himself, Joey could not stop his revelations to Higgins, who was the only friend he had.

"Lots of times, he'd hold my head down in the trough. Or he'd whup me where it never showed. But tonight he hit me with his fist, real hard, and knocked me down."

"Why?"

"My ma lost her baby again, and he said it's my fault and how she doesn't want me and that's why she keeps trying."

"He's lying through his teeth," Higgins said. "You got to know that."

Joey only knew his unbearable hurt. "He said if I ever came back, he'd kill me. And you can't tell anyone I was here, or he'll shoot you down. Don't never tell nobody we was friends."

Realizing the boy was rattling on and hysterical, Higgins tried to reason.

"Maybe it's just talk?" Higgins asked, moving the stew pot to the side on the stove.

"I seen him do it, and he even kicked the dead guy."

Higgins agonized, trying to think of ways to calm the boy. "Did you talk to your ma about this?"

"No, she's sick all the time, and that mean old housekeeper is always there."

"I can get the sheriff."

"He won't do nothing. He's afraid of my pa. Everyone is."

Higgins fretted. "I've seen him and your ma drive through town, and fellas get out of sight real quick. So I've heard that same kind of talk, how he's killed maybe a dozen men. Except they say the fights are always fair and square."

"He's so fast, nobody ever has a chance."

"So why would they draw on him?"

"I seen him do it. He moves his hand like he's gonna pull his six shooter, so they go to draw first, and then he beats 'em." Joey readily drank the hot coffee that Higgins offered him.

"But why does he even go after them?"

"My ma's Uncle Jed pays him."

"Uncle Jed?'

"Jed Creighton. He stole my ma's ranch down in Texas."

"How do you know that?"

"I know how my Grandpa Ben left it to her, and she ain't got it no more." Joey felt great relief to finally tell his only friend the secrets he had been hiding.

"You leave tonight, you'll get lost out there," Higgins worried.

"Rain stopped and the moon came out, so it's okay. Just a real bad norther."

Higgins limped to the window to peer out, then came back. He had to swallow the news as best he could, and it pained him that this boy had been carrying such a load for so long. His own childhood had been rich with love of family and never with such turmoil.

Higgins moved to the iron stove where the stew pot steamed. "Well, you're not leaving till I get some hot food in you and make sure got what you need."

Glancing at his heavy rifles, Higgins declined to even offer one to such a small lad, but he would worry. "So all this is why you made me promise never to tell anyone you was working here?"

"Yeah, cause I don't want you dead." Joey felt his aching jaw.

One thing Higgins didn't tell Joey was that his wages came out of Higgins own pocket, just to help what he saw was a miserable little guy. Now he was learning why, and he knew the knowledge would haunt him forever.

Higgins bit his lip in anger and thought, *If this boy was mine, I'd be so happy, my boots would never touch the ground.*

"I ain't never coming back." Joey took the offered food and ate hungrily despite his sore jaw. "And I'm gonna change my name. I ain't Joey Lassiter no more. My middle name's Ben after my grandpa, so that's gonna be all I keep."

"So, Ben…"

The boy looked at a silver cross on the wall. "Ben Cross, but don't never tell nobody. Promise."

"You got my word, son." Higgins fretted. "You need money?"

"No, I got all my wages saved up."

As Joey/Ben Cross, wincing in jaw pain, finished the hot stew, Higgins persisted.

"Why would a father hate his own son?"

"I think it's the money. The ranch got stole, but I heard how my grandma left my ma a whole lot of money in some bank in St. Louis, and she gets some every month. And then if she's gone, it only goes to her 'issue' or something like that, which is me. So as long as I'm around, he can't get it."

Higgins worried. "But how will I know you're okay?"

"You won't, and don't worry, but you can't tell anyone I was here."

"You have my word on that," Higgins promised.

Joey/Ben wiped his mouth with his sleeve. "Someday I'll grow up and be bigger than him, and I'll have a gun so fast, I'll make *him* run."

Higgins didn't argue. He just figured the boy was hurt and scared and saying things to make himself feel better.

Later that same night at the rail yard, the newly named Ben Cross, wearing his slicker, mounted his aging bay in the moonlight and high wind. His old saddle creaked. His newly-filled canteen and food sack hung from the horn. Behind the cantle were his belongings and a bedroll Higgins had given him, along with some matches wrapped in a pouch, which he pocketed.

He waved goodbye to the worried Higgins and rode northeast into the night.

Higgins limped back into his shack and settled down with his collection of newspapers. Starting at a headline, his vision blurred as tears came.

"Dear God, please take care of that boy."

* * * * *

Northeast of Denver City, some two days later in occasional rain and constant wind, young Ben Cross rode in open country until he reached the south side of the wide, flooding South Platte River. He continued east along its path.

Normally more shallow with a muddy bottom, the storm had sent a raging current down from the Rockies with debris that spun and hurled along the way. The banks were lined with the occasional cottonwood, sometimes a tired willow, and an abundance of heavy, rambling brush.

The wind grew wild and heavy, whipping him under a darkening sky. Oftentimes it showered, with wet getting inside his collar and icing his already chilled skin.

Determined, he hunched down in the sudden downpour just as lightning struck nearby. His horse jolted, bucked, spun and fell sideways, hitting the muddy ground before leaping back up. Shaken but having landed free while still holding the reins, Ben staggered to his feet. He loosened the cinch on the jittery horse as it shuddered.

The wind whirled debris around him, even as the rain turned back to drizzle.

Drenched, he could only hover on foot along the bank, next to an unfriendly pile of brush under a lone cottonwood, where he tethered his weary mount. Unable to build a fire with wet brush, he drew his slicker to cover him all the more and bent his head as wet poured off his hat brim. He slept off and on.

At first light in another drizzle of rain, he awakened to see riders at a far distance, coming from the direction of Denver City. Moving along the south bank of the wide, raging river, they could not see him or his horse because of the trees and heavy brush.

Frantic, he got up, threw his belongings behind the brambles, untied his old bay and tightened the cinch poorly. He got on board and rode his reluctant bay into the wild river, desperate to cross the raging water to the other side where there was more brush and trees for cover.

His bay sank, rose, fought the muddy, sandy bottom heavy with silt that dragged it down to the mercy of the current.

As Ben frantically grabbed at the animal's mane, the saddle slid sideways, dumping him into the current as debris hit him full force.

Thrown deep into the river, Ben lost his grip and ended up on his own, splashing about. His hat fell back to the chin strap. He tried to reach his horse but failed as it sank, rose, and moved on without him downstream while fighting to get to the far bank.

Barely able to save himself, Ben fought his way back to the south bank where he had entered the water. His scarf had come loose and now hung on the brush above the river. Realizing it would lead to the belief that he had drowned, Ben tossed his hat onto the same branches beyond the water's edge.

Knowing the riders could soon spot him, he crawled directly from the river into the thick brush as it tore at him. He made his way close to where he had hidden his possessions. He had lost sight of his horse as it moved downstream.

The seven approaching searchers, bent forward as rain poured off their hats and slickers, were led by Lassiter. They rode up and studied the scene in the pouring rain. One hand dismounted to wade deep enough to retrieve Ben's hat and scarf, then handed them up to Lassiter, who managed to hide his pleasure.

"Check downstream," Lassiter said.

Watching the men ride east along the river, their backs to him, Lassiter smirked.

Ben, shaky and soaked to the skin, kept low in the brush next to his belongings. His skin crawled. He choked on his own breath. Terrified Lassiter would hear any sounds of his agony, he bit his lip and scrunched up. The thorny brush had scratched his face and hands. He felt no pain in the cold wet because his fear was more powerful.

When the men finally returned, one of them told Lassiter what they had seen.

"That old nag made it to the far bank with the saddle under its belly. Right then and there, it just dropped dead."

Ben shivered in the brush and watched them, worried they would camp as he silently prayed. *Please, make them ride on back, get out of here. Lord, I sure could use a little more help.*

Lassiter put on a show of grief and tugged at the brim of his hat. Lassiter hid his secret joy in Joey's demise—all because that little boy had been an aggravation since the day of his birth.

"Sorry, boss," one said to Lassiter. "We could camp and look for him come morning,"

"No chance he'll ever be found now." Lassiter's pasted a sad look on his face. He spun his horse. "His mother will need me. So let's go."

Miserable in the heavy rain, the men turned and followed him back, west along the river.

Ben breathed a painful sigh of relief. *Pa can't hardly wait to go home and tell Ma I drowned. And I got no horse, but I can walk, because I ain't never going back.*

He shivered, felt the cold wet of the river through his clothes. He managed to pull off his boots to drain them, and rubbed his near frozen feet before pulling them on again. He knew that in his bag, hidden in the brush beside him, he had dry clothes, but decided the rain would just soak him through again. He pulled his slicker back on, over his wet clothes, and could not stop shaking with chills. He continued to pray.

Back at the rail yard in the wind and only a mist of rain as the day grew long, Lassiter, hiding his glee, led his men along the tracks and headed toward town.

Of a sudden, afternoon sun brightened the yard.

From in front of his shack, Higgins painfully recognized the boy's hat and scarf tied to the pommel of Lassiter's saddle. Sick inside, Higgins wiped his eyes with the back of his hand, glad he was unknown to Lassiter.

One of the searchers, Andy Boggs—a fifty-three-year-old Lassiter ranch hand—reined up on his own as the others, not missing him, rode on to town where they would soon hit the saloon. Boggs turned his horse and rode over to dismount near Higgins's shack. He tied up at the post.

Higgins held open the door, welcoming Boggs inside.

Unknown to Lassiter or the other hands, the two men had formed a friendship whenever Boggs came to the yard to pick up ordered supplies. Checker games had become frequent. Boggs had never seen Joey/Ben working at the yard and had no hint of Higgins knowing the boy.

Shutting the door on the rain, Higgins, sworn to silence, limped to the stove as Boggs removed his slicker. Higgins poured them hot coffee as they sat down on creaky chairs.

"We been up river searching. Seems this boy ran away a couple days ago." Boggs said, shaking his head. "Tried to cross the river and drowned."

Higgins, startled, fought back his tears and stared into his cup. There was nothing he could do, but he hated being helpless and unable to speak about his lost friend. He would keep his promise, but he had trouble hiding his painful grief.

"What boy was that?" Higgins asked.

"Harry Lassiter's." Boggs sipped his coffee and made a sour face.

"But why did he run away?"

"His pa hated him."

"Why would a father hate his own son?" Higgins blurted.

It took a long moment for Boggs to answer. He sipped his coffee.

Higgins could barely contain his secret as pain shot through his chest. Then finally Boggs enlightened him in a way Higgins could barely handle.

"Because the boy ain't his."

Higgins stiffened, held his cup in both hands to stop them from shaking. "What?"

TWO

When the Lassiter search party returned with the news that Joey/Ben had drowned, Andy Boggs stopped off at the guard shack to get out of the rain. Hanging his slicker inside by the door, Boggs shared coffee with his secret friend Higgins. They sat by the hot stove as Higgins ached with the startling news, not only of the drowning of his young friend, but about Lassiter.

With rain and wind pounding the shack, Higgins fought back his tears.

"What did you say?" Higgins persisted.

"I said, Lassiter hated the kid because he wasn't his son."

"My God."

Smoke seeped from the chimney, causing Higgins to pause long enough to limp over and open the damper. He hustled back to his chair and took up his coffee cup. He shivered down to his boots with the news.

Boggs continued. "Nobody around here knows, and the boy had no idea, but I was there, down in Texas when it all happened. Working for Jed Creighton's outfit. The boy's ma—

she's Jed's niece—she was forced to marry Lassiter because she was carrying."

"So who's the boy's real father?"

"Tom Landry. In Huntsville for life, for murder."

Higgins waited, but he soon realized Boggs would say no more. And, he thought painfully, it was all too late. Digging at the truth now would be of no help to a lost boy. Or to Higgins.

"How about some more of that coffee?" Boggs asked.

"Yeah, sure."

* * * * *

Early the next day in drizzling rain, Ben Cross—no longer Joey Lassiter—walked east along the south bank of the raging waters of the Platte. Hatless, he wore his slicker and carried his belongings. He had wrapped a sack around his head, but it didn't stop the wet. At twelve and small for his age, having suffered more than his fair share of ill treatment, he had only his courage to keep him going.

And his prayers.

He could not stop shaking from the chills and, late in the day, found shelter under some big cottonwoods and brush near the bank. He tried to build a fire to no avail, even though the clouds were breaking. It was then he looked up in the drizzle to see a rider coming from the south on a black horse and reining up to look down at him.

The elderly man had a white beard, kind gray eyes that twinkled, a wide brimmed hat pushed back from a well-lined brow, and wore a yellow slicker. He had a bedroll and possibles on the back of his saddle, along with a rifle in his scabbard.

He seemed friendly, causing Ben to stand up at his grin.

"Hey, young fellah. Looking for work?"

Ben couldn't speak as he nodded.

"We're moving a herd up to Montana Territory, and we need hands. So, you ever work cattle?"

Ben shook his head but he began to feel excited with new hope.

"Well, you get your gear and hop up behind me," the man added. "A little hard work will put some meat on you."

Ben, a sudden grin on his face, could not believe his good fortune, and quickly gathered his possessions. He would give thanks in prayer for the rest of his life.

Hoisted up behind the stranger, Ben hung on for dear life. He pressed his face against the man's slicker and never looked back.

From then on, Ben found a home among tough cowpunchers, joking waddies, and wild cattle—some longhorns from the wiry brush of Texas, others crossed with Red Durhams and only slightly easier to handle.

From the old timers, he learned a lot of history, including from men who fought on both sides of the War Between the States. He also learned that a real man would stand by his word. That integrity was highly prized. They taught him to handle troubles with a sense of humor.

"If you learn to laugh at yourself," one said, "you'll live a lot longer."

Ben learned to ride like a Comanche, rope anything that moved, and how to shoot a rifle, but never as good as the ole hands. At local fairs and on the Fourth of July, they were dead-eye shots, and often winners. Ben never had that knack with a rifle.

Many times, he would dream of his mother's sweet smile, but the nightmare of his brutal father destroyed any memories he would have chosen to treasure. At times, he remembered the kindness of Higgins, but he could never put his friend in danger by contacting him.

When he turned fourteen, Ben had saved enough to buy an Army Colt, and it fit his hand so well, he never missed a shot. From then on, he became dedicated to practice his aim and quick draw, soon updating his weapon to one with cartridges. Some of the hands shared his enthusiasm, seeing it as fun. Ben saw it as being ready for the day he might have to face Lassiter once again.

Ben also vowed no one would push him around, not anymore.

Surprisingly, he grew and grew until he was a good six feet tall. Hard work and chuck wagon grub gave him muscles, big shoulders, and welcome strength. But it was his fast draw that soon won contests and made the old timers grin. They also enjoyed his big size.

"You were a little runt when we found you," one said, "and now you could wrestle a grizzly."

And if I ever see my pa again, he'll back off, Ben told himself.

At local fairs and dances, a teenage Ben was leery of trusting any of the young ladies that gave him that come-hither smile. The old timers had not given him a clue on what the heck he was supposed to do, so he always ran.

At one particular Fourth of July celebration in central Montana Territory in 1876, Ben—now a handsome nineteen year old—once again won the fast draw contest in the final round, shooting three ink bottles before they hit the dirt.

The old timers cheered his win, which was a new saddle blanket, and as Ben collected it from the judge, he paused to admire the colorful weave. A deep voice from behind him broke his thoughts.

"Son, you're in the wrong business."

Ben turned. He stared first at the silver circle star that read UNITED STATES MARSHAL, MONTANA TERRITORY shining on the grizzled man's black leather vest.

Ben hardly caught his breath before he found a star on his own vest and learned a new trade from the seasoned lawman.

* * * * *

In the spring of 1877, a twenty-year-old Ben continued his life as a lawman, considering it his new home, and wished often he could write Higgins, but he knew he could not put his friend in danger. He was unaware of events unfolding in Denver City at the same time.

Under an overcast sky, Andy Boggs rode to the Denver rail yard to tell Higgins, still his secret friend, the latest news over coffee. In his guard shack, Higgins, graying and still lame, had his usual pile of newspapers and a hot fire in the stove where they huddled.

"I've been riding for Jed Creighton's brand since I was a kid, and I guess I'm too old to change," Boggs said. "Even with Lassiter running the show up here, I got no place else to go." Boggs sipped his coffee, then leaned back in his chair. "But now, seems Creighton got fed up with carpet baggers down in

Texas and all them new taxes. Plus some of his water supply got fouled with that black gooey stuff coming up from underground. So he done sold out and is moving his herd and all of us up to Simmons Flat in Montana Territory. On account of all that free grass."

Higgins hesitated. "Lassiter going along?"

"You can bet on it."

"And his wife?"

"Yeah, sure. He never lets her out of his sight."

"And I heard they have a housekeeper."

"You mean the jailer? No, she ain't going. Too darn old."

Higgins pondered the news. "Well, I hope it goes well for you."

"I got no family, no kinfolk. I reckon when St. Peter calls, I'll still be riding for the brand. You find a home, you kind of stay with it."

"Like me with the railroad." Higgins remembered Ben's warning that rainy night so long ago. "One thing I got to know, Andy, you ever mention my name to Lassiter?"

"No, and not to anyone else."

"Thanks."

"I'd never let you be a target." Boggs grinned. "Besides, you spend all your time in this dirty old shack. You ever go to town?"

"Not much. Too dang populated."

"Yeah, and you sure have a soft job."

"I earned it. I once got shot up pretty bad guarding an express shipment." Higgins downed his coffee. "Oh, I get around okay. Just some misery in my right leg. Fellas here keep me supplied with grub and coffee. And books and newspapers. And wood for my stove." Higgins gestured. "What more does a man need?"

"Not much, except a woman."

"Had one once. She died in childbirth, both of 'em, before either of us turned twenty."

"Hey, that's rough."

"And that was it for me."

"I've known lots of women," Boggs said, "but I figured my horse and saddle, my rifle, that was enough. So here I am an old bachelor with nothing more to show for it. And yeah, I have a home with the outfit, but I got my regrets, on account of Lassiter. Everyone knows what he does for Creighton, but nobody got guts to say it out loud. Especially me."

"Well, sir, I hope Montana Territory is a better place," Higgins said.

"Maybe so."

"You could write," Higgins suggested.

"Can't hardly write my name," Boggs said, "and besides, I don't want you tracked down and shot on my account. But I may be back someday when the winters up there get too cold."

Higgins, saddened by his friend's leaving, tried to remain cheerful for Boggs' benefit.

* * * * *

In 1879 Montana Territory, Ben, at twenty-two, continued to find his way as a Deputy U.S. Marshal. He learned enough law to keep out of trouble. He was given great freedom as a roaming deputy, but he also concentrated on eastern Montana Territory where trouble makers came in from hiding out in the Dakotas.

In early March of 1880 with a snowy winter still lingering, Ben visited his friend Jack Hayes—the middle-aged County

Sheriff Hayes, whose office was in the small cow town of Gorman's Creek. Hayes wore a graying handlebar mustache and a black leather vest.

Over coffee by the hot stove in the sheriff's office one night, they played checkers with Ben winning more often than not. The oil lamp flickered, making them both sleepy.

They were interrupted by the skinny bartender at Pike's Saloon. He hurried inside out of the cold to warm his hands. In his shirt sleeves, he shivered as he spit it out.

"The Hogans, all three of them, in my saloon! Drinking real heavy. And they stink like they ain't never been washed."

Suddenly alert, Ben finished jumping Hayes' checkers, then adjusted his hat and stood up to pull on his coat, as did Hayes.

Hayes stretched. "All three are wanted."

"I know," Ben said, "but this is the first time they came out of hiding."

Hayes loaded two double-barreled shotguns and handed one to Ben. "Let's make this short and sweet."

The bartender followed them outside into the cold night.

Inside the saloon, the lamps burned bright. Card players had moved as far away from the bar as possible.

Standing with his gaze on the mirror that hung on the back wall behind the walnut bar, Zeke Hogan—the oldest and meanest at forty with a trim black beard—downed his whiskey, looked around for the missing bartender.

Bo and Bart, Zeke's grizzled younger brothers, in that order, reached over the bar for bottles. All three were heavily armed with right-handed draws, and looking mighty dangerous. They were also feeling their whiskey. All three were dirty and smelled as if they had been sleeping in the wrong part of a barn.

Now they glanced in the smudged mirror.

Two double-barreled shotguns were aimed at them from just inside the swinging doors. The three wanted men turned with sneers, raising their hands slowly.

"Well," Bo said, "looky here."

"Yeah," Bart said, "an old man and a kid marshal."

Men still in the saloon scattered even further from the line of fire, many scurrying out the swinging doors and scattering into the night.

The three Hogans kept their hands up, but not so high—they might be foolish enough to draw. All three were intoxicated, slowing them down.

"One false move and you're dead," Hayes warned.

The Hogans hesitated, weighing their chances.

Hayes and Ben both looked ready to fire as they moved closer, too close for the men to draw but not close enough for the lawmen to lose control of their scatter guns.

"Drop your gun belts, with your left hands," Ben ordered.

The Hogan brothers hesitated, but finally surrendered and dropped their gun belts.

"There'll be a next time," Zeke said, burning their faces into memory.

* * * * *

At the rail yard in Denver in late March of 1880, Higgins, now sixty-nine, gladly received newspapers from a conductor friend and returned to his shack to read them. Rain pounded the roof and wind shook the walls of his shack.

Sitting in one chair with his feet on the other, Higgins

scanned a week-old Montana paper. To his surprise, he saw an article that brought him to the edge of his chair as he stared at the words:

> **March 10**: Notorious outlaw brothers, Zeke, Bart, and Bo Hogan, wanted for armed robbery, rustling and murder, were arrested in Gorman's Creek, Montana Territory, just last week. Arresting officers were Sheriff Samuel Hayes and Deputy U.S. Marshal Ben Cross.

Higgins felt a sudden jolt of unbridled joy. Then his heart sank as he realized it was impossible. No one could have survived trying to cross that raging river, especially not a skinny little kid. He knew that. And yet, he sorely wished it was true.

Higgins kept staring at the brief item, then finally shook his head. Just an old fool's daydream.

* * *

Then weeks later, Higgins read another item:

> **April 5, 1880 - Deer Lodge, Montana Territory**: Brothers Zeke, Bo, and Bart Hogan have been sentenced to one year confinement for armed robbery. Other charges were dismissed due to lack of evidence and missing witnesses.

Higgins just shrugged at the light sentence.

At the same time, he was unaware that the following year

would bring a startling chain of events that would uproot him forever from the comfort of his lonely shack.

*   *   *   *   *

The year 1881 began with sad news.

On a cold night in May, Higgins—still at the rail yard in Denver—received an unexpected letter from a Deacon Jones with no return address but postmarked Butte City, Montana Territory.

He settled by his hot stove in the guard shack and had his curiosity satisfied in a painful way. He opened the letter and stared at the neatly written words.

> Dear Mr. Higgins,
> On May 8, 1881, your friend Andrew Boggs died of natural causes in Simmons Flat, Montana Territory. He had asked that I relate his lasting friendship and farewell to you. Please do not reply to this letter as it would put both our lives in danger.
>
> Regards,
> Deacon A. Jones

Higgins could not figure why the deacon from Simmons Flat—now known as Hang Town—was afraid, or why the letter was mailed in Butte City. It made Higgins all the more glad that Andy had never revealed Higgins' friendship to anyone. Regardless, he was sad, missing his friend.

Nights with checkers and a chance to just chew the fat with Boggs had given Higgins a great deal of pleasure. They had told stories and jokes, had remembered olden days. At times they had just sat together, watching the coffee steam on the stove, listening to the wind and rain, or dozing in silence.

Now he felt a deeper loneliness as tears brimmed in his eyes. *Goodbye, Andy, and yeah, I know you cheated at checkers when I wasn't looking, but you know what? You were my only friend.*

Except, he thought further, *for the little kid I will never forget.*

Meanwhile an urgent, special delivery letter was being hand-delivered from Butte City via Wells Fargo Messenger to the Superintendent at Huntsville Prison in Texas.

THREE

At Huntsville Prison, Texas, May 12, 1881, a young and weary Wells Fargo Messenger entered the office of Superintendent Thomas J. Goree with Summers, a curious aide, close on his heels.

The messenger reached inside his coat for a leather pouch.

A handsome, bearded man who had practiced law, Goree had been with the Confederacy but now had settled into a more peaceful life, doing the best he could at the prison, including offering worship services, a library, arranging basic education and a mill inside the walls to teach a trade and give the men work satisfaction. The prisoners operated and published a newspaper. They also worked outside the prison on loan to pay for prison needs.

Grand paintings in oils of the West, complete with Indians and trail herds, hang on the walls of Goree's walnut-paneled office, along with antique rifles and pistols.

The Wells Fargo man handed over a soiled, fat letter.

"Who's it from?" Goree asked.

"It's sealed, but it came down from Butte City, Montana

Territory, and only can be delivered to you, personally."

Goree signed for the letter and then waved them both out of the office, his curious aide closing the door behind him.

Alone now, Goree opened the sealed envelope and saw a folded paper with a note from Emmett T. Long, County Sheriff, Simmons Flats, Montana Territory, dated May 8, 1881. Goree stared at the enclosed dying confession in neatly printed words and a shaky signature with the name Andy Boggs below it. Witnessed by the sheriff and a Deacon Jones.

After reading every bit of paper, a fascinated Goree stepped out of his office and called to Summers.

"Get me an appointment with the governor."

Back in his office, Goree sat in his chair and shook his head. Long-time prisoner Tom Landry was a Texan and deserved better. Goree felt he would find ready assistance from Governor Roberts, also a former Confederate and a loyal statesman.

Texans had to take care of their own.

On May 15, 1881, the prison superintendent returned from Austin where he had met with Governor Roberts. He stood behind his desk with more papers in hand.

He called in Summers. "Where's Landry?"

"He was in the mill, but I think he's gone back to the newspaper."

"I want to see him. Alone."

Before long, a grizzly old guard brought Tom Landry to the superintendent's office.

Goree waived the surprised guard back out, bidding the door be closed behind him. He then gestured for Landry, who was not bound in any way, to sit in front of his desk, after which Goree also sat facing him.

Tom—once a skinny teen on arrival, and now a big muscular but lanky man nearly six feet tall—had not been in the office since he himself helped restructure and modernize it. Now at forty-three, his hair was still dark brown but with gray streaks. With a trim graying beard and mustache, wearing prison garb with a Trustee tag, he had no idea why he had been summoned. He sat fondling his right hand, which was bound with bandage.

"What's with your hand?" Goree asked.

Tom's voice had become deep over the years, not just with an even stronger Texas drawl, but deep with restrained emotion. "It acts up sometimes. Hurt it as a kid, trying to pound a horse shoe with my left hand."

Goree took this in, but he had something more on his mind.

"You've been a model prisoner, Mr. Landry. You've helped others to find relief in hard work. They learned smithing skills from you. What's more, you've taught many of them to read and write. You've read every book you could lay your hands on. You sing in the choir, and do sketches of the men to send home. You're a self-educated man, and you should be proud of that."

Tom, basically shy, shrugged with embarrassment.

Goree leaned forward with a document-sized folder in front of him.

"I received a letter from the county sheriff at Simmons Flats in Montana Territory. Place they call Hang Town. Sheriff Long, he said of the three men who testified against you, only one was still alive. The sheriff took down his dying confession, witnessed by a deacon. It seems all three lied at your trial."

Tom felt a chill run through him. Anticipation now became painful. After twenty-five years in prison, could this really be happening?

"The sheriff's letter and the confession are in the governor's safe, but I have here a copy of both, printed on one of them new fangled typing machines. They can't leave my office, but you can read them for yourself."

Tom wanted to reach out and grab the papers, but he restrained himself.

"The dying man said they gave false testimony st the time out of fear for their own lives." Goree set the folder on the desk. "In fact, we've since learned you were the only suspect in the murder. There was no trial transcript, just that the judge sent you to prison instead of an execution because you were only eighteen and a recent orphan whose father had fought with Houston at San Jacinto."

Tom nodded. "My father was the best man I ever knew."

"I'm sure he was." Goree hesitated, then took out the typed papers. He handed over the copy of the sheriff's letter first.

Tom suffered as he read it to himself:

> A dying man gave me this signed confession in the matter of the murder of Amos Creighton in 1856 in West Texas. He said he and two other ranch hands gave false testimony against a Tom Landry in fear of their lives but would not say more of the threat or who made it. He asked that I tell no one except you. It seems you may very well have an innocent man in prison. However, I must offer caution if you free Landry. The Creightons moved up here from Texas.

> Jed Creighton owns the biggest cattle ranch around and has an army working for him. His niece is married to his hired gun, Harry Lassiter, reportedly the fastest draw west of the Mississippi.

Tom winced, a pain jabbing at his chest.

He had often wondered what had happened to the sweet young girl he had loved with all his heart, knowing she had only abandoned him because of her uncle's tyrannical control. He had received notice of the annulment and bore no resentment on that, because not only was he sent to prison for life, but he knew she would have had no say about any of it. But why did she marry Creighton's hired gun?

Tom reluctantly returned the sheriff's letter to Goree, who now provided the typed copy of the confession, saying, "It was originally hand written at the dying man's direction, but signed in his own name as Andy Boggs."

Tom stared at what it said:

> To save my own life, I falsely testified in 1856 down in West Texas and sent a kid named Tom Landry to prison when maybe he was innocent. Now the doctor says I got a bad heart and I'm dying, so I got to say I was one of three ranch hands forced to swear we saw Landry at the barn the night Jed Creighton's kid brother Amos was shot in the back and robbed inside of it. The other hands are dead now, so I got to tell how we lied on account of we was off night-herding at the time.

Tom blinked back stinging tears, wiping his eyes with the back of his hand, then reading further.

> All the other hands and the boss was out after rustlers at the time, but the boss said they found Amos' money sack in Landry's saddle bags, so we figured maybe the story we told to save ourselves wasn't that far off, but I was mighty grateful he didn't hang. Just the same, our lies helped send that kid to Huntsville for life. We don't know if he or someone else did the killing. And I ain't gonna say no more on account of when Landry gets out, he oughta go to Mexico and stay there.
>
> (Signed) Andy Boggs

Tom returned the page, reluctantly. He remained badly shaken.

Goree straightened, lifted out an official, gold-embossed paper. "We take care of our own in Texas, so the governor issued a full pardon. As of now, you are a free man. This is an official copy to carry, but the original is held by the governor. And because of leaks from his office and this prison, our public record will only show you are now paroled on our work-release program. You'll check in at the KC Ranch, where we had you breaking broncs for a time. In fact, KC said you could put a rein on a horse better than any man he had ever seen."

Tom swallowed hard at the compliment, which he savored.

Goree continued. " He said you could whisper in a horse's ear and it would jump through hoops." He paused to grin at Tom's reddening face before adding, "And he'll personally make sure you're outfitted. He'll put out the story you're one of six men driving horses to south Texas. "

Tom choked on his gratitude. "Thank you, sir."

Goree handed him the official copy of the original pardon, along with an envelope for carrying. Tom took it in his hands, staring at the current date of May 15 and the governor's signature with the gold seal.

Goree himself had difficulty staying calm. "We can wait a few weeks before informing the newspapers, and we will then say the pardon will be issued and signed on July 1. We decided that if you had a hankering to head for Montana Territory, it'd take a month or more to get up there, especially since I'm told they had more snow this season than in all their history, and flooding is already a problem. With luck, you might be up there by late June. But they won't be expecting you for another month after that."

Tom stared at him with such dismay, that Goree smiled.

"Tom, I just explained, we take care of our own in Texas." Goree reached out to Tom with a bank draft, which was accepted. "The governor came up with three hundred dollars, the best he could do. But it'll give you a fine start."

Tom Landry placed it all in the envelope, but remained in a state of shock.

"Now, a bit of advice," Goree said. "You came here as a teenage smithy. You became a skilled carpenter and have made a good show running our newspaper. Now you could do the same on the outside. Or teach school. And find a girl and get married."

Tom felt his breath tighten. "Yes, sir."

"You have a chance for a new life," Goree said, "so don't

throw it away on a vendetta. It's okay to look for the truth of it, but don't end up in another prison."

"No, sir," Tom replied out of respect, but held up his bandaged hand to offer the injury as proof he wasn't going to carry a side arm.

Goree got the message but worried. "Remember now, if Jed Creighton finds out who you are, and if he still blames you for his brother's death, your life will be forfeit, so I hope you have a plan."

Tom nodded, thinking, *yes—to keep my mouth shut.*

Tom gratefully held the folder with the pardon and when the superintendent stood, Tom got to his feet and offered his hand, which Goree took with great admiration for his long-time prisoner.

* * * * *

Tom faced a whole new world, a freedom that tasted sweeter than he could have possibly imagined. The green grass and air smelled so clean, the sky seemed bluer, the stars more bright, all so overwhelming, he could barely handle it. He gave thanks by the hour.

After being outfitted at the KC Ranch, Tom took the old rancher's advice on the best way north. He moved northwest across Texas on horseback in mid May of 1881, crossed the swollen Brazos by a rickety ferry, and saw the rail tracks building west before he turned himself north along the panhandle with Montana Territory a long way ahead. He knew he had time, as no one would expect him until late July, but he did feel an urgent need to move along as best he could. He avoided towns, trains and stagecoaches, preferring the loneliness of the prairie.

He carried a sidearm in his saddlebag, but with his bad right hand, had no plan to use it. He also had a Winchester '73 repeating rifle in his scabbard. He wore black clothes because it suited his mood, but at the same time, sported a new twenty dollar black Stetson with a wide brim, and new shiny, black Justin boots with blue trim on the uppers.

Still wearing a short graying beard and trim mustache, he never expected anyone could recognize him after twenty five years, especially not with his size and build. He rode a Texas double-rigged saddle on his bay gelding. He led an aging gray pack mule loaded with newly acquired needs for the long trek north.

Along the way at lonely camps on the prairie, he practiced firing his rifle, finding he had deadly aim with an okay trigger finger. However, because of a teenage accident with a forge, his right hand remained slightly crippled, making it unlikely he could ever hold a revolver, nor could he aim well with his left hand.

North along the prairie while camped at twilight, he tried again with the revolver in his left hand, hitting everything but the target. At the sound of his gunfire, prairie dogs would pop up, take a curious annoyed look, then disappear into their homes.

"Okay," Tom would grin and say to them, "so I was a better smithy."

As nights fell and he looked up at the glittering stars, Tom had yet to get used to such freedom. He gave thanks constantly and prayed he would make good use of this turn of events, and not have to kill, or be killed. He fully expected trouble if he was recognized, but he would fight to keep this glorious return to life.

At the same time, he wondered if the sweet Leslie he knew had been changed by marriage to a hired gun. He felt in no hurry to face the truth. It would be painful enough just to be reminded she was lost to him forever. Yet he could not stop his headlong charge into history.

* * * * *

On June 14, 1881, at the Denver Rail Yard, settled in the guard shack for the evening, Higgins took out the two-day-old Texas newspaper he had just received from a yard worker. Wind rattled his shack, returning smoke, forcing him to use the damper.

By lamplight, his stocking feet propped up on a box, he opened the paper. He scanned it and turned the page. He picked up his cup of hot coffee, only to jump and spill it on himself with a yelp, and then bring his feet back to the floor.

He stared at the item with amazement. "My God! A pardon for Landry?"

He read the short announcement over and over. He knew that, innocent or not, Landry would be headed for Hang Town once he was pardoned on July 1. If there was any chance that Ben was alive, he had to be told.

Higgins began his urgent mission. He had barely a month to act before Landry made it to Montana Territory.

Sending a letter by messenger to U.S. Marshal Botkin in Montana Territory, he wrote that he had serious and urgent family news for a Ben Cross who would be about twenty-four years old. The marshal's return letter clearly confirmed his deputy was that age and was working out of Gorman's Creek. The same Ben Cross who had arrested the Hogans.

"Can it be?" Higgins fretted aloud to himself. "I got to know for myself, in person."

With no warning to anyone, Higgins hurried north by rail to Cheyenne and then a pounding, miserable journey by stage to Montana Territory, and then east. At a lonely relay station, he bought an old nag to ride the rest of the way south to Gorman's Creek.

* * * * *

Late June of 1881, on a sunny morning in Gorman's Creek, the normally quiet little cow town appeared half asleep. Then, sudden gunfire burst from the lone saloon on the north side of the empty street.

At the same time, Higgins walked out of the stable on the west end of town and stopped on the south side of the street, unnoticed as he pulled his hat brim down to shade his eyes from the overhead sun. He could see onlookers appear, then back into doorways.

Staggering out of the lone saloon on the north side of the street, Matlock—a drunken, fifty-year-old, huge grizzly of a man—laughed and waved his six-guns. He fired at the sky.

Matlock stumbled about, yelling, "Yahoo!"

His hat had fallen back and dangled from his chin strap. Rust-colored hair stuck to his head like a sheep's behind. Wearing shaggy pants and shirt, he was a fun sight to behold as he staggered in circles, still laughing.

Following him out of the saloon, two rumpled, middle-aged

and shaggy saddle tramps with sidearms looked ready to shoot him down.

Out of the café across from the saloon walked Ben Cross. Now twenty-four years old, he wore a Deputy U.S. Marshal's circle star on his black leather vest, and twin holsters. Husky, over six feet, handsome, clean shaven, Ben tried to keep a straight face.

Higgins, staring in disbelief, shook his head. He decided there was no chance this big fellow had any resemblance to the skinny little kid he remembered. Disappointed, he could only stand and watch the drama.

Matlock spun, laughed, and fired crazily into the air. One of his guns clicked, empty. He turned at the sight of the saddle tramps and threw the empty weapon at them. It landed on the boardwalk at their feet.

The two aggressive men were not intimated by Ben's badge, seeing him as just a kid too big for his britches.

"He cheated at cards," the bigger man snarled at Ben.

The other reached for his six-gun, half-clearing leather before he froze.

Ben's revolver had sprung into his hand with lightning speed and was aimed at the two men.

The man trying to draw let his weapon sink back into its holster as he and his partner, equally dismayed, began to back away.

"So this drunk cheated you?" Ben snapped. "More likely, you were trying to roll him. Now get out of town and don't come back."

Buffaloed, the two men turned to claim their horses at the hitching rail. They mounted and rode east up the street, soon on the open trail.

Higgins, still doubting this was the same Ben Cross, stood watching in silence.

Once the saddle tramps were out of sight, Ben turned his attention to the big drunk dancing around in the street.

Matlock, still laughing, his back to Ben, fired his other weapon and hit a store sign across the street with another yell. "Yee-haw!"

Ben came up behind him, raised his boot, slammed it into Matlock's rear end, sending the big man falling crazily forward, who landed on his belly with a big thud.

Matlock rolled over and sat up, laughing heartily, but could not get to his feet.

Across the street, Sheriff Hayes, his star shining on his tan vest, ambled out of his office wearing a big grin under his handlebar mustache.

"Thanks, Ben. I would hate to have to shoot the old fool."

Matlock sat looking silly, still full of giggles.

The sheriff caught up Matlock's now-empty weapons and helped Ben get the big man to his feet. It took all their strength. Hayes shoved the guns in Matlock's holsters for temporary transport. He then cuffed Matlock's hands behind him.

The sheriff marched the laughing Matlock across to the jail and inside.

Ben grinned, then crossed back over toward the café. As he stepped onto the boardwalk, a voice from his right startled him.

He turned to see but did not immediately recognize the seventy-year-old Higgins with his graying hair, white beard and mustache, and floppy, stained hat, facing him on the boardwalk while favoring his right leg.

"Ben Cross, is it?" Higgins asked, uncertain.

Ben hesitated, cautious.

"Maybe you used to work for me," Higgins said, limping a step closer and daring to ask. "At the yard. In Denver? Sweeping out warehouses?"

Ben suddenly got the message. "Mr. Higgins! My God, is that you?"

Higgins, startled, choked on his sudden joyful tears at Ben's standing there, alive and well and having survived against all odds. "Sure is."

Ben, shaken that his past had reared up in his new life, still happily took Higgins hand in a hearty grip. "God Almighty."

Men had come out of doorways with the excitement now over, but they either sat in the shade down the street or went back into the stores or the barber's.

Higgins, catching his breath, looked around to be sure no one was in earshot. "You sure are a surprise. And look at you! Big as a barn."

Ben grinned, backing away. "How did you find me?"

"Well, sir, last year, I read about this hot-shot deputy marshal named Ben Cross capturing some outlaws. I figured it was just a fluke because you was supposed to be dead. But then all of a sudden, something came up I couldn't just sit on, so I took a chance and wrote your boss. Then I heard back and he said yes, you were maybe twenty-four, and also that you were the best man he has."

"Glad I still have a job. You tell anyone?"

"No, but how is it Lassiter and them thought you'd drowned?"

"My horse nearly did, getting to the far bank, where it died."

"But you..."

"It dumped me in the river, and I was able to make it back to the bank. Hid in the brush."

"Thank God. But you were okay out there, all alone?"

"An old timer with a trail herd picked me up, made a cowhand out of me. Until I got too big for my britches and ended up with a badge."

"Yeah, but what happened to that skinny little runt of a kid?" Higgins shook his head in amazement. "You got to be at least six feet."

Just then Matlock came roaring back out of the jail, laughing, waving one cuffed hand. He staggered into the street. The sheriff, roughed up, came clumsily out of the jail.

Ben turned to hurry over and confront the noisy Matlock. The big man charged with open arms as if to hug Ben, who leaped aside and tripped him. Matlock landed on his belly with a loud "*oof*," the wind knocked out of him.

Matlock laughed, got up, spinning around as Ben snapped the dangling cuff back onto his other wrist. Ben turned him around, marching him up onto the boardwalk and into the jail. The sheriff followed. Inside, the loud clang of a cell door was followed by more laughter.

Ben came back outside and over to Higgins, shaking his head as they grinned at each other.

"Glad you didn't hurt him," Higgins said.

Ben gestured. "Come on, my coffee's getting cold. And you look hungry."

Higgins painfully swallowed the news he had carried all the way from Denver.

As he followed Ben to the café, he rehearsed over and over how he would tell his friend about having an ex-convict for a father. Even worse, how Hang Town might be headed for an explosion.

FOUR

Inside the small café that late morning in Gorman's Creek, Ben and Higgins were the only customers. Sitting near the window, both had apple pie and coffee, enjoying themselves and their history as they grinned at each other.

The old waiter cleared the table and refilled their coffee cups. They waited until he headed back to the kitchen.

"Sure am glad to see you," Ben said. "Still with the railroad?'

"Yeah, but they just keep me around for old time's sake."

"You know, it took a lot of years before I could look back, and I figured out that when I was sweeping out the warehouses, you were paying me out of your own pocket."

"Somebody had to look after that skinny kid," Higgins said with a wry smile.

Then Higgins sobered, fingered his cup as he remembered how he had grieved when he thought the little kid had drowned. He was finding it difficult to match tiny Joey with this huge lawman. He dabbed away a tear.

Ben tried not to be as emotional, but he'd never forgotten the kindness of this man, his only trusted friend. He sensed this was not just a reunion of comrades.

"You must have a good reason to come all this way," Ben said.

"I do, yeah."

Ben pushed his hat back. "You look like you're busting to say something."

Higgins felt his throat go raw and dry. Words were going to come hard.

"So?" Ben prompted.

"Well, it sure ain't easy. Especially since you're so big. Geez." Higgins paused with an emotional sigh, then shook his head and began. "First I got to say, that six-gun leaped into your hand out there. One minute it was in your holster, then—*pow*!—it was in your hand! How did you get so darn fast?"

"Practice." Ben hesitated. "Has anyone been following you?"

"No, and ain't nobody else knows you're alive. Or why I'm here."

"And I sure don't." Ben studied how serious Higgins looked.

It took awhile for Higgins to prepare. He was about to startle, upset, even agitate his young friend. Moreover, Ben was no longer a skinny little kid. He was a big man with a badge. A likeable, easy-going lawman who could take care of himself. Higgins cleared his throat.

"Well, a few years back, your ma's uncle, Jed Creighton, he sold out in Texas and took everyone north, including everyone in Denver. Up to Simmons Flat, over to the far west of this here territory. Got their hands on half the open range, I hear. And they call it Hang Town because of the vigilantes."

"I heard of it."

"Anyway, that's where your mom is."

Ben felt a wrenching tug in his heart. "How is she?"

"Sickly when she left, but that's all I know."

Ben stared into his steaming coffee. He had loved his mother, and maybe she had felt the same, but that witch of a housekeeper had seen to it they were never alone from the time he was four years old. His mother's bad health and his father's threats had kept Ben from raising a ruckus around her. Not to mention a twelve-year-old boy being told over and over that she didn't want him.

Higgins sipped his coffee, then leaned back. "That brings me to the rest of it. And I got no choice now."

Ben waited, feeling a sudden dread at Higgins' painful expression.

Higgins steeled himself, working up to what he had to say. "I had this friend Andy who worked cattle for Creighton on Lassiter's place in Denver, and he was with the search party that went looking for you. So when everyone said you had drowned, Andy up and told me something, and it all seemed too late then. As far as I knew, you were gone. So I just swallowed it. Like a bitter pill. But all of a sudden, I got more news, and that's why I'm here. It's about Lassiter."

Ben grimaced as his father's name ground in his stomach, forcing an explosion of repressed memories. The abuse in the barn, the threats, the nights he couldn't sleep for fear Lassiter would someday drown him in the trough, the spells of violent coughing when allowed up from the water, all memories he had buried until now.

"I don't care a plug nickel about him," Ben said.

Higgins hesitated. There was no other way to say it. Yet he had to force his words to come out loud enough for Ben to hear.

As he spoke, he watched for Ben's reaction.

"But he ain't your real father."

There was a long pause as Ben started to sip his coffee but set it down. The startling revelation suddenly made the past more understandable. Ben thought, *thank God*, and smiled as if it lifted a huge burden, then sobered as it hit hard. He looked at Higgins' sincerity and concern.

"Why am I not surprised?" Ben asked. "But who is, then?"

"Andy told me his name was Tom Landry. In Huntsville for life. For murder. Down in Texas. But since we both thought you had drowned, he had nothing more to say, and me, I was all broke up and didn't ask to hear anymore. I believed it was just too late."

Ben gripped his cup and waited in painful suspense.

Higgins paused to lean forward. "After that, it just sort of set in my craw that you never knew the truth. Then all of a sudden, I saw this in a Texas newspaper. So I figured I'd better take a chance you really was alive and track you down."

Higgins handed the newspaper clipping to Ben, who stared at it:

> **JUNE 12:** A full pardon will be issued and signed July 1, 1881, for Thomas J. Landry who had been convicted in 1856 of murdering Amos Creighton. No other information was forthcoming.

Staring at the short item, Ben could hardly breathe. "My God."

"I have no idea what really happened."

"And my father doesn't know I exist?"

"Not likely. I figure after Landry went to prison, Miss Leslie found out she was with child, and that had to be when she was real young. So her uncle Jed Creighton, he forced her to marry Lassiter and move up to Denver."

"So, my real pa was innocent?"

"We don't know that. The paper doesn't say nothing else except that he got a pardon. Maybe they just figured after twenty-five years, he'd served enough time. Or maybe he's sickly. Could be anything."

Ben stared into his coffee, a lifetime of anger showing in the tremor of his young hand. He looked at his shaky fingers, pressed them onto the table to make it stop. "But he's down in Texas. Will he stay there?"

"Can't be sure, but if I was in his shoes, innocent or not, I'd be looking for Jed Creighton. What's worse, when they learn Landry's out, Lassiter'll likely be lying in wait." Higgins downed his coffee. "And that's why I'm here. I figured you had a right to know."

Ben reflected. "It'll take him a month or more to show up. I've got to get there ahead of him and get some answers."

"Well, it's for sure no one will know who you are, because you're supposed to be dead, and on account of you're so big and husky now. But that badge will make you a target. They don't call it Hang Town for nothing."

"It'll stir things up." Ben downed his coffee, and both men readied to leave. "I'll pick up my gear at the boarding house, but that won't take long."

"I had to buy an old nag to get here from the stage, so I hope they got some for sale at the livery."

"No need, I have my own string boarded, but I'm riding

hard. Maybe you're too old for it. And you could get hurt being tangled up with me."

"I'm going with you, and that's it."

Ben turned, hurrying outside and walking fast with Higgins hustling to keep up. Ben steamed in the hot sun. "Lassiter hated me because I wasn't his own son. And that's why he kept after my mom to have more kids."

"And why he lied, saying she didn't want you."

"Yeah, it took me a lot of years to figure you were right, that it was a lie, but all that time he was beating on me, I never got to know my real pa. What a dirty rotten trick."

Yeah, Higgins fretted silently, *but suppose your pa ain't no better than Lassiter?*

By mid afternoon, they were headed west on the trail that would lead to the stage road. Ben rode a chestnut with a creamy white mane and tail. Higgins rode a sorrel. A chunky bay pack horse carried their gear.

Ben meant business with his twin single action Frontier Army Colts and his Winchester '73 repeating rifle with matching .44-40 cartridges. He felt he had spent his life getting ready for this day.

Higgins, only carrying a rifle in his scabbard and no side arm, worried he may not have done Ben a favor with this revelation. Seeming to have a good life, Ben sure didn't need to run into Lassiter again. Yet, a boy should be able to meet his true father.

They crossed swollen rivers and creeks, suffered a stormy day of hail the size of an egg, visited lonely army posts for a few nights, and continued as fast as their mounts were able, ever heading west. Pronghorn antelopes, tan with white bellies and rumps, danced across the grassland. Most nights, coyotes howled at the moon.

Often, they would see a red-tailed hawk sailing high while inspecting its terrain.

Another day, a sudden north wind whipped the tall grass into a frenzy before driving them to shelter at the ruins of an old fur trading fort. After which, an icy chill followed them.

"We get there," Higgins said by the campfire one night on their journey west, "I'll say I'm scouting business for the railroad which is still stuck in the Dakotas."

"And I'll be there to investigate the vigilantes."

"We better say we just met on the trail."

Ben nodded and stared into the flickering fire, wondering if his father was guilty, and if he had kinfolk, and what kind of man he might be. Maybe it didn't matter, because no one could be worse than Lassiter. Yet a boy needed a father, and he had been denied that comfort. Worse, he had been kept from his mother's side. It all seemed so darned unfair to a little kid, forced to run from it all and dare to live on his own in a world that would ever be strange to him.

He began to wonder more and more about how he would feel to once again see his mother's lovely face. At the same time, he struggled with bitter hate that could give him away when he saw Lassiter once again.

With the past unresolved and the future in doubt, Ben had to pray for help. Now more than ever in his life as a lawman, he had to keep his head, be in control of his every move, and not give himself away until the time was right.

He lay back in his blankets and looked at the stars sprinkling the vast black of the heavens. He closed his eyes as a lone coyote howled in the distance.

Across the firelight, Higgins hurt for his young friend and dreaded what might happen in Hang Town.

* * * * *

Two days after Ben and Higgins left, Sheriff Hayes let Matlock out of the cell at Gorman's Creek late morning. The big man had an enormous headache but tried to ignore it as he loaded his six-guns. Watching, Hayes figured he would not be shooting anyone for real.

"That was good grub," Matlock said of breakfast. "Now I got to talk to that kid marshal."

Sheriff Hayes frowned as he sat at his desk. "Why?"

"If it wasn't for him, I'd be dead, on account of them two fellahs was gonna have my hide. I owe him."

"They said you cheated at cards."

"Hey, I couldn't even see straight." Matlock donned his hat. "So where's the kid marshal?"

"He's gone. West to Hang Town."

Matlock adjusted his gun belt. "Hang Town? Where the vigilantes are? He's gonna need me."

"If you stay sober."

"Hey, that was just a toot." Matlock held up his hand. "Trust me."

Sheriff Hayes laughed.

* * * * *

Ben and Higgins continued west until they came to where another stage road intersected from the south and pointed north. They reined up at the wooden sign indicating a right turn but shot full of bullet holes and leaning sideways. The name **SIMMONS FLAT** was crossed out and **HANG TOWN** written in big black letters in its place.

"Not good," Higgins said.

Wondering what they were riding into, they continued north where tall waving grass, flashing shades of green, and scattered brush spread to their right and far ahead, with rising red bluffs to their left.

To the far west, the snow capped Rockies rose high above where scattered mining camps were known to be dug into the foothills and cliffs. Still riding in the open, they could now see woods and red ridges rising ahead of them.

One morning, they reined up on the trail to rest their mounts. Higgins turned in the saddle, taking a good look at Ben, his admiration obvious.

Higgins gestured at Ben's revolver. "I guess you really are pretty good with that hog leg. But I figure if Harry Lassiter's still alive, there's a good reason, so he has to be just as lightning-fast as he ever was. And he don't play by no rules."

"I know that."

"I'm not telling you what to do, but I spent all these years thinking you was dead, and I'm getting too old to do that again."

Touched, Ben just smiled and nodded. Higgins had been his only friend back in Denver City. His respect for the man would always include having seen him as the only real father figure that skinny little kid had been able to embrace.

Continuing north toward cattle country and wide spread open range, they saw more and more of the red bluffs and dense woods closing in on their left.

Ben's anticipation ranged from seeing his mother for the first time in twelve years to wondering how he would handle his rage when he saw Lassiter, not to mention the possible arrival of a father he never knew existed.

Now they saw a turkey buzzard circling far over and into the red canyons. Black with a naked red head, it would glide for a time, then rapidly flap its wings before sailing again.

* * * * *

Two days behind Ben and Higgins at twilight on the stage road north, Matlock spotted Tom's campfire in the trees, a hundred yards on the left.

Tom's fire burned small but bright next to his saddle and gear. His bay gelding and pack mule stood in the trees away from the camp, near the creek. Tom had moved into the dark with his rifle, standing out of sight. He watched the big man ride closer.

Coffee steamed on the rocks by the fire. Beans filled a frying pan off to the side.

Riding into the firelight on his sorrel, Matlock reined up, pushed his hat back.

"Hello to the camp!"

No response. Matlock started to dismount.

Tom's deep voice came from the trees. "Hold it."

Matlock, staying in the saddle, called out. "Hey, mister, I'm no trouble. I just smell your coffee."

Still unseen, Tom said, "Step down. Leave your gun belt."

"Yeah, sure."

Matlock dismounted, unbuckled his gun belt and hooked it on the horn. He took time to loosen the cinch on his weary sorrel. Walking close to the fire, he paused, not a bit worried for some reason, maybe instinct.

Tom lowered his rifle, came into the light, and squatted by the fire. He waved permission to the big stranger, who grinned happily.

Matlock sat near him, legs crossed. "I'm Matlock."

Tom nodded, didn't volunteer a name. He poured them both some coffee, but he didn't take the offered hand. "I'm not shaking hands with a big oaf like you. I could end up standing on my head."

Matlock chuckled. "I know a Texas drawl when I hear one, and that sure is a Texas saddle, so is it okay to call you Texas?"

Tom, amused, nodded.

"You're a long way from home then."

Tom tried to be careful. "Just got out of the army in the Dakotas. Spent the last year in a hospital."

"You must be glad to be outta there." Matlock looked to the hot pan of beans. "Sure am hungry."

Tom nodded to a plate. Matlock helped himself.

The big man finished, took up his coffee. "Me, I'm from Kentucky. Didn't have no folks. The church had a bunch of us, but they said as how I ate too much. So I run off when I was high enough to ride a freight. Worked for some farmers. Then a couple cattle ranchers. Never could stay in one place for long."

Tom, enjoying the story, refilled their cups with steaming coffee.

Matlock continued. "Over in East Montana, I wanted to marry this girl, but she laughed at me. So I went on a toot and got in a lot of trouble. But this kid marshal got me out of it and locked me up."

Tom saw no connection to his own life, but the big man was entertaining.

Matlock grinned, then sobered. "Anyhow, I heard how this kid marshal was headed for Hang Town. I figure it ain't called that for nothing. So I'm gonna get up there and look after him. What about you?"

"I'll ride along."

"Good. I've been talking to myself for days. Mind if I unsaddle?"

"Water in the creek back there."

After Matlock cared for his horse and tethered it near Tom's bay and pack mule in the trees, he put his saddle and bedroll down near the fire.

The big man sat down with a grunt and grinned at Tom. "What about you? Got a wife and kids?"

"Nope." Tom poured more coffee. "What do you know about Hang Town?"

"I heard it's cattle country and they're expecting the railroad to come across from Dakota, maybe this year, so they already got corrals for shipping. But there's a big fight over the open range. And there's been rustling, and that's where the vigilantes are."

"You're well informed."

Matlock laughed. "No, I got this from the sheriff who had me in jail."

Tom liked the big man and felt no threat from him.

"You mind?" Matlock asked, pulling a harmonica.

"Nope, just keep it soft and low."

"I'll take first watch."

"Thanks, and do you know Red River Valley?"

"Sure do."

Yet, even as Tom laid down in his blankets while Matlock played softly on his mouth harp, it was difficult to fall asleep for a long while. Too many questions about what happened in West Texas. Too many painful memories. Wondering how he would feel when he saw Leslie after twenty-five years and how he would handle seeing her married to a hired gun. He didn't remember Lassiter, but he sure recalled Jed Creighton shaking a noose at him.

A coyote howled far away. A critter scooted at the edge of the campfire.

Tom finally drifted off.

Matlock lowered his harmonica. He liked the Texan.

Pouring himself more coffee, Matlock felt peaceful. Even the lone coyote's renewed howl was friendly to him. He looked up at the clouds moving across the starry sky.

Matlock bowed his head to say his night prayer.

FIVE

Ten miles west of Simmons Flat—now known as Hang Town—lay the entrance to the vast acreage of the Creighton Ranch, which also had claim to most of the wide open range to the east and spreading ever north with tall, waving grass sometimes emerald, other times whispering blue.

The ranch boasted of seemingly endless, rolling green hills with scattered herds of cattle and horses as far as the eye could see, north and northwest. In the near west rose high, wooded hills with colorful displays of wild flowers, including Indian Blankets with their red and yellow daisy-like flowers.

To the distant west, the snow capped Rocky Mountains sparkled in the sun.

Ranch headquarters was surrounded by gentle hills in its own little valley, while a range of thick woods, red cliffs, and canyons fell to the south.

Away from the barns and corrals, off by itself, stood a grand two-story white house with a veranda around the second floor and a grand porch surrounding the first level. Facing the front entrance, a very wide and colorful flower garden spread behind a white picket fence.

Unseen from the front view, a kitchen area had been built behind the house to keep odors from inside, and further back, the servants' quarters.

On that sunny Saturday afternoon, two ranch hands—one redheaded and twenty, the other freckled and late teens—remained on the ranch to work colts in the far corral north of the house and next to the biggest barn.

As the freckled hand struggled with a colt, the other laughed. "You'll never make a hand if you keep that up."

At that point, the colt spun free and the youth went flying against the fence. The colt danced away, tossing its head. The red-haired hand kept laughing.

Not far away stood a red buggy barn, set off by itself, with a bay gelding in its own corral. It faced the garden but at a distance.

Over at the house and in the garden, Leslie Lassiter—forty-four and still lovely with dark green eyes and light brown hair—stood alone. Appearing frail and sad, she wore a light blue jacket over her blue print dress and held a single red rose in her gloved hand. She looked to be carrying a load on her shoulders that would never go away. A woman without hope.

Leslie turned and quickly smiled when she saw Suellen Long riding up on a golden palomino mare with flashy white mane and tail. Riding side saddle in green riding skirts and jacket, Suellen reined to a halt at the garden gate and near a big stump just outside the fence. Her long, blonde, wavy hair framed her pretty face and covered her shoulders.

Dismounting with her black boot on the stump, Suellen then draped the reins on the fence. Just turned twenty-two, she looked fresh and pretty. She was bright, full of life, compassionate, and educated, and yet her shining blue eyes and smile hid a lonely life. She came into the garden to greet Leslie near a bench, on which they both sat with Leslie to her right. Suellen drew a folded newspaper from inside her jacket, revealing her holstered revolver, just out of sight and strapped to her waist.

"Here's your Texas newspaper." Suellen handed it over. "I hope it's the right one. I'm sorry it took so long to get it. The barber rescued it from his necessary."

Leslie removed her gloves and noted the date on the heading.

"Yes, this is it. June 12."

"Do they always hide it from you?" Suellen asked, leaning back.

"No, this was the first time." Leslie, sitting stiff and upright, glanced at the headlines in the newspaper, then turned the page.

Suellen watched her search the articles.

They both paused to look around to be sure they were alone, but they were not.

Peering out the big front window, Emma Creighton—fifty years of age but still glamorous in blue silk with her done up dirty-blonde hair—parted the curtains a little wider to be sure they knew she was watching. Emma's pretty but hard, tight features were set in grim disapproval.

"Oh, dear. There's your Aunt Emma."

Leslie nodded but continued looking through the paper.

"Why do you share a house with her?" Suellen asked, abruptly. "I think it would be miserable."

"My husband said it was safer for me, because I've been sickly."

"She's always so mean looking. Does she ever smile?"

Leslie shrugged. “Only when she wants something from my uncle. He’s never been able to say no to her. When he’s around, she’s sweet and affectionate with him. That’s why she has a room full of Paris gowns.”

“So she has this grand palace with servants, and lords it over the whole valley.”

“She does put on a show,” Leslie agreed, turning a page.

“I’ve never been invited to her teas,” Suellen said, trying to ignore Emma’s stare.

Leslie concentrated, still searching the paper in the bright sunlight.

Suellen tried to cheer Leslie. “The Fourth of July is on Monday. It’ll be my first time while living up here, and I hope it’s as much fun as it was in Kansas. Maybe you can share some of it with me?”

“I’m sure we’ll be there for the celebration, but I’ll probably have Emma watching my every move. I can’t even enjoy going to the store and just looking at ribbons or buttons. Or a new bolt of cloth. She’s my shadow.”

“Maybe you could at least go riding with me now?” Suellen asked.

“No, I’m sorry. Ever since this newspaper came, I’m not allowed to leave.”

“So, now you want to know what’s the big secret?”

Leslie suddenly sat up straight, staring at an inside page of the newspaper.

“My God.”

“What is it?” Suellen asked, leaning close and staring at the same words as Leslie pointed.

> **JUNE 12**: A full pardon will be issued and signed July 1, 1881, for Thomas J. Landry who had been convicted in 1856 of murdering Amos Creighton. No other information was forthcoming.

Leslie's eyes brimmed with hot tears.

Worried, Suellen put her hand on Leslie's arm, felt her shivering. "Yesterday was July 1. But who is he, and how did he end up in prison? And then get himself a pardon?"

"It's been a secret all these years," Leslie said, tears spilling over. "Oh, Suellen, I have to tell someone, but it can't go any further. You have to promise me."

"No, it won't, I promise."

Tears trickled down Leslie's face as she whispered, "I was married to him."

Suellen, startled, took her hand, and squeezed. "I didn't know."

Leslie sobbed, wiped at her eyes, tried to ignore Emma, and turned her back as much as she could to the window, leaning closer to Suellen. Her words reflected her painful memory and endless sorrow.

"I was barely seventeen and he was a year older when we met at the Fourth of July picnic in West Texas. On the dance floor, and no one noticed because I had a lot of dance partners. He was an orphan, working for the smithy and doing odd jobs, so my uncle would never have found him suitable. We met secretly after that when I would go riding."

Suellen stayed silent as Leslie continued with her tearful story.

"We had only known each other a few weeks, but we were in love and decided to elope."

"That was brave."

Leslie nodded. "I snuck out my bedroom window at the ranch that night. My Uncle Jed and most of the hands were still tracking rustlers on the border, and the men left behind were out night herding. Tom was to meet me up in the big canyons around midnight. I waited all alone, for hours, and Tom finally came at daybreak. He said he had trouble rounding up the money for us to get away. He said the smith he worked for was so drunk, he finally had to leave without his last week's pay."

Suellen waited, aching for Leslie as her story continued.

"We were married in Three Corners on the way north."

"So it was legal."

"Yes, but my uncle Jed was my guardian and tracked us across the border into New Mexico Territory. Three days later, he surprised our camp at sunup. His men took Tom prisoner and kept him away from me."

Leslie winced. "That's so bad."

"Uncle Jed decided Tom must have followed my Uncle Amos, Jed's kid brother, from town and into the barn the same night I had run off, that Tom had shot Amos in the back and robbed him. My uncle said some of the men had come in from night riding and seen Tom that same night riding away from the barn."

Leslie wiped her tears before continuing.

"He said they found Amos' money pouch in Tom's saddlebag. And a pistol."

Always suspicious, Suellen made a face. "They could have been planted on him."

"Yes, but either way, Tom would have been hanged on the

spot, except my uncle forced me to agree to an annulment and never to see or contact Tom ever. So I had no choice. I had to agree to an annul our marriage to save Tom's life. My uncle hid me away, and I never saw Tom again."

"And you're sure it was annulled?"

"A lawyer had me sign it and some other papers I didn't understand."

Suellen frowned, her imagination spiraling. "Did you think Tom was guilty?"

"No, never. He was such a sweet, kind boy with a big heart. He couldn't even step on a bug."

Suellen bit her tongue and thought, *Yes, sure, like the kindly churchgoer with little grand kids who decided to shoot the parson and three others before he was jumped. Or the really sweet young man who ravished a rancher's daughter and left her for dead. And that lovable nice old man who had bodies in his basement. Or the little old lady who spiked her cookies with rat poison and left them as secret gifts on folks' doorsteps.*

A sheriff's daughter, Suellen had seen life the way Leslie had not, but she tried to be kind. "No one else was around when you left the ranch that night?" Suellen asked. "No one heard the shot in the barn?"

"Emma said she was upstairs in the house asleep and didn't hear anything. And the housekeeper was also asleep at the far back of the house on the first floor and said she heard nothing."

Suellen waited, squeezing Leslie's hand as she continued.

"After that, I was locked in my room for weeks with a guard outside my window. Until Tom went off to prison for life. I know they sent the notice of annulment to him. Must have been awful for him, on top of everything else."

"I'm so sorry." Suellen paused. "But now he's out and got a pardon, so maybe he will come up here, just to find you."

"He must never do that. My husband would never let him live."

"So, it's true that your husband kills people. Why isn't he in jail?"

"He always has witnesses to swear they're all fair fights."

Suellen couldn't help herself now. "Can I ask, why did you marry a man like Lassiter?"

"After Tom was sent away, I learned I was with child."

"My gosh, so…"

"I was forced to marry."

"A hired gun?"

"I was only seventeen. My uncle was my guardian. I had no one else. No friends, no one. He said Harry was smitten with me and would be a good husband. He ordered us to a ranch near Denver where I gave birth, but Tom's son died when he was twelve."

"I'm so sorry."

"Harry always wanted a son of his own. Except I was sickly every time I tried to have another child, and I needed help, so Harry hired a housekeeper."

"I'm so sorry. What did the doctor say?"

"To stop trying, but my husband…" Leslie shrugged it off. "After losing Tom's son, I was so unhappy, I ran away when the housekeeper was asleep, but Harry dragged me back and kept his men watching me. And they still are."

Suellen glanced toward the front window. "Emma is watching us now."

"She always does."

Suellen tried to be gentle. "So they didn't want you to know

Tom Landry was out of prison, and that's why they hid the paper from you. Now she can see I brought another. Maybe I'm in trouble."

Leslie shook her head. "No, not while your father's county sheriff."

"Leslie, I have to ask. Where was Lassiter the night Amos was robbed and killed?"

"They said he was in town."

They both pondered the thought.

"But," Leslie said, "my uncle sent for him to join in the search for me and Tom."

Suellen hesitated. "Would you even recognize Tom if he came here?"

"No, I don't think so. We were so young. And it's been twenty-five years followed by a lot of sickness, so it's all a blur."

"Emma's still at the window."

"Please, don't repeat any of this," Leslie urged. "Especially not to your father, because then he would want to do something."

"Don't worry. I won't say a word." Suellen hesitated. "Besides, he went to Butte City three days ago and hasn't returned."

"Are you worried?"

"Always, but he's been a peace officer since before I was born, so you get used to it." Suellen adjusted her hat. "My mother died when I was four, so he's everything to me. We were last in Kansas, but before he came up here, he said it wouldn't be safe, so he sent me east to stay with my aunt, and she put me in finishing school."

"I can't see you in finishing school," Leslie said, wiping at her eyes.

"I know which fork to use and what to wear and how to do whatever high society women learn, like being a real lady and a grand hostess. I studied art, slept through the symphony, and can quote Longfellow and Emerson. But I was a misfit, and I ran off in a huff. And left that iron corset hanging on the garden gate."

Leslie felt grateful for the story as a distraction. "I wish I could go to a symphony and sleep through it. Do you miss any of it at all?"

"No, I'm much happier being around my father, but the vigilantes have started doing his job for him. I've tried to get him to leave, but he won't listen. And now he's trying to get me to marry just about anyone who'll take me far away from this place."

"Have you someone in mind?"

"Are you kidding? I haven't met one man who doesn't wet his britches if he's anywhere near your husband or your uncle. If I ever do, I'll marry him on the spot. But Hang Town's not going to change, and I can't leave my father to face it alone."

"So, we're both stuck." Leslie flushed. "But I'm glad you're here. I have no one else to talk to. You have to know, you're my only friend."

"It means a lot to me, too." Suellen adjusted her gun belt, half hidden under her jacket, before continuing. "But it's so dangerous. With open range, there's always some cowpoke wanting to brand a few mavericks. That's why they hang so many north of town, in the black canyons where the big old trees are. And it's not just your uncle's doing. All the big ranchers are secretly paying the vigilantes."

"I only hear these things from you."

"Don't repeat them or I won't be welcome here."

Leslie carefully tore out the small item about Tom Landry,

slipped it into her pocket, and then folded the newspaper before setting it aside, all the while with Aunt Emma watching.

"I should head out," Suellen said, glancing at the afternoon sun.

Leslie handed her the single red rose.

"Hey, thanks."

They stood up and Leslie walked with Suellen to the garden fence, where Suellen paused to hug her before opening the gate.

"I'm sorry I can't ride with you," Leslie said. "Are you going straight back?"

Suellen walked through the gate to her palomino mare. "No, I'm riding down through the red rock canyons where they reach the south road to town. But I'll be circling back to the north road where my place is."

"It seems out of your way."

"It's a lot prettier. And there'll be some wonderful wild flowers that like the shade of the trees."

"I envy you."

Suellen retrieved her mount, reins in hand. "As soon as I water my horse. Maybe borrow a handful of grain."

"Of course." Leslie then frowned. "But I worry about you riding alone."

"Don't," Suellen said with a smile as she opened her jacket to show the pistol in a holster at her belt. "I'm a very good shot."

"Now I really envy you," Leslie said with a smile.

Suellen gave her another hug, then turned and led her horse to the trough and a grain bin by the buggy barn before mounting and riding away, south.

Leslie picked up her gloves and went back to pruning a rose bush. She pretended not to see Aunt Emma still at the window.

Emma watched the lovely Leslie with envy and years of anger, her own secrets more troubling than Leslie could imagine.

* * * * *

That same Saturday afternoon, as Leslie began her ride south, Ben Cross and Higgins rode northwest on the stage road and in sight of the same red rock canyon. A busy little stream came bouncing out of the narrow passageway and found a new pathway in the rocks to their left.

As they neared the canyon entrance, they reined up short.

They watched the same turkey buzzard they had spotted from the stage road. Now it circled lower and lower to the canyon.

"Same old buzzard, ain't about to give up. May be a varmint," Higgins said, "but this being vigilante country, maybe we oughta have a look."

They rode left on the narrow trail into the canyon, maneuvered around stray pines, oaks, and brush, and near the little trickling creek. All of a sudden, they saw the tall cottonwood not fifty feet away to their right, its seeds casting bits of snow among dark green leaves in the light breeze. Dangling from a high limb, a mustached, middle aged man, no longer alive, wore a sheriff's star on his vest.

Overhead, the vulture continued to circle.

There were no other ropes on the tree or marks, making it appear this was a new location for a lynching. No one else was around. No sign of the dead man's horse.

Marks of horses' hooves in the dirt headed back the way Ben and Higgins had come.

Ben leaned over to look at the prints. "Maybe three of them."

Higgins frowned. "We can't ride around this. We have to take him to town."

Higgins dismounted. Ben rode up and leaned over to cut the rope with his knife.

Higgins lowered the body, and Ben dismounted to help him.

The vulture sailed off to a distant rock on the bluff and perched, waiting until it found something more interesting beyond the canyon wall and flew away.

"They left the star," Higgins said, "but they took everything else. You can see the watch fob still dangling."

"You sure you want to keep wearing your star?" Higgins asked, worried.

"Yes, even more so."

They were unaware that the sheriff's daughter would soon be riding on the scene.

SIX

That afternoon, deep in the woods of the red rock canyon, Ben Cross and Higgins lowered the hanged sheriff to lie on the green grass.

Higgins knelt and searched for papers, anything, but only found the star on the man's vest.

Taking down his bedroll, Ben planned to retrieve a blanket.

"My gosh," said Higgins, still kneeling but gesturing north up the canyon."Will you look at that?"

Ben followed his gaze and let the bedroll hit the dirt.

They could only stare at the grand and golden apparition, as Suellen came riding out of the far woods side saddle on her dancing palomino mare. Beautiful with her flaxen hair flowing free around her shoulders and carrying a handful of flowers, she rendered them speechless.

Gorgeous, stunning, she seemed from Heaven and like no one Ben had ever seen in his life. *Wow*! Ben thought, not even sure she was for real.

Wow! was Suellen's first thought, too, on seeing Ben from a distance.

The men tipped their hats. The polite greeting kept her from being afraid of them.

As she came closer to them, she reined up, clearly startled at the sight of the prone dead man lying on the grass some twenty feet away. An older man with a mustache and a star. She put her hand over her mouth to stifle a cry but it escaped with a gasp.

Higgins agonized. "Ma'am, this ain't no place for you."

Ben quickly rolled out his bedroll to retrieve a blanket.

Pain in her chest, shivers down her spine, she was shattered. All her life as a sheriff's daughter, she had suppressed her dread of this day. Now it was here, and she let her tears run down her face, unheeded. She choked on a sob.

Ben hurriedly spread the blanket over the sheriff.

She took sudden stock of the circle star on Ben's vest as he faced her, while she stayed in the saddle. She felt the elderly Higgins' fatherly concern in his kind gaze as he approached on foot.

The wild flowers and rose spun from her hand to flitter down to the sandy trail.

She swung down, dropping the reins, leaving her mount ground-tied. She trembled and sobbed with her words. "I'm Suellen Long. That's my father."

Tearful, shaken, she started toward the body but folded some six feet away.

She sank to the ground, her hands over her face as she wept. Her skirts heaped around her. She became suddenly hysterical, gasping for breath.

Higgins came to her side and went down on one knee. "My name's Higgins. And the marshal, here, he happened to come along when I did. And I'm sorry, but they took everything your father had, even his watch. Except for his badge."

She sobbed and seized his hand.

"We'll take care of him." Higgins hurt for her. "You got some place to go, some friends?"

She glanced at the blanket covering her father. She looked away quickly. She allowed Higgins to help her stand. She leaned on him as his arm went around her. She wiped at her eyes and gestured back north.

"The Creighton Ranch. It's just over the ridge. I need Mrs. Lassiter to take me home. Our place is on the north road to town."

The names hit Ben hard, but her trauma dwarfed his own.

Higgins worried. "Are you sure you can ride?"

She nodded, as he helped her over to her palomino.

"I'll see you get to the ranch, and the marshal can wait till I get back."

Higgins paused to see if Ben wanted to take her, maybe see his mother after twelve years, but Ben didn't offer. In fact, he noticed that Ben remained speechless.

"Then," Higgins continued to Suellen, "we'll take your father to town and get word to you of the funeral."

Suellen whispered her thanks as Higgins helped her astride on her side saddle.

Higgins nodded to Ben. "I won't be long."

Ben watched as Higgins mounted and rode north in the canyon with Suellen. He grimaced. *What kind of a place is this? They hang a sheriff. And that girl, she lost her father. What else lies ahead?*

And then out loud to himself, "My mother's up there on that

ranch. But if I see Lassiter now, I may give myself away before I'm ready. I figure I'd better know the odds and the lay of the land."

As Ben waited in the canyon, Higgins and Suellen rode northwest over the ridge and down toward the Creighton Ranch. Higgins saw it as a well laid out spread. He noted the grand house with its flower garden and white picket fence.

Higgins also saw the two young men working a colt in the far corral near the big barn. They glanced his way, hesitated, then went back to work. No other hands were in sight, on the ranch or where the cattle and horses grazed on the far green slopes, backed by wooded hills.

He and Suellen rode up near the garden gate. He swung down and then helped the tearful young woman safely to the ground.

Leslie, still in her print dress and jacket, but wearing a sun bonnet, came through the garden toward them. She removed her gloves and hurried to the gate and out to greet them.

Higgins saw how lovely she looked. *So this is Ben's mother. No wonder Lassiter keeps a tight rein.*

Leslie hardly noticed Higgins, a stranger to her, as she hurried to her friend.

Suellen fell into Leslie's embrace and sobbed. "They hanged my father."

"I'm so sorry," Leslie whispered and started to cry.

Higgins tipped his hat to Leslie. "My name's Higgins, ma'am. We'll be taking the sheriff to town. And we'll have them send word to wherever she lives as to when they'll have the funeral, so no need to go to town until it's set."

"We?" Leslie questioned.

"A young fellow came along same time I did. He's helping."

"Please," Suellen said to her, "can you help me get home?"

"Yes," Leslie said quickly, without glancing back at the house.

Higgins started to mount his horse, but Leslie called to him. "No, please wait. We need your help with the buggy."

There was no question Leslie and Suellen could hitch up a buggy, so Higgins sensed trouble. Hat in hand, he stopped short of mounting. He gestured toward the buggy shed. "Want me to tell one of the hands to hitch up your rig?"

"They won't do it," Leslie said. "They won't let me leave."

"Please help," Suellen said, wiping her tears.

"Yeah, sure," Higgins said.

He lead the way to the shed with the palomino and his horse trailing. The buggy shed had its back to the corrals, so the hands could not see what they were doing. Only Emma at the front window was aware.

Higgins retrieved the bay horse from the corral and hitched it to the rig. He tied the palomino on lead from the rear. He knew the buggy could never navigate through the woods in the canyon, but he worried about them being on their own.

"You'll be okay?" Higgins asked them.

"Yes," Leslie said. "We have to go directly east, over that hill and across the flats on the north road."

"Do you need to go back to the house?" Suellen asked her.

"No, I'll have to go as I am. She'd try to stop us."

"I can always shoot her if she tries," Suellen said.

Higgins, amused at first, then sobered at the gun belt and holster under Suellen's jacket as she spread it open to make her point. "Any more law in town?"

"There's a deputy," Leslie said.

Higgins worried about Suellen. "Are you all right now?"

"I will be, as soon as we're out of here," Suellen said, noting the young hands in the corral could not see the buggy as yet, but that Emma was still at the front window.

Suellen sat up on the left side of the seat as Leslie climbed in on the right to take up the lines. They would have to make a run for it.

"We'll be okay now," Leslie assured Higgins, only because she didn't want him hurt or even shot in a confrontation with the hands. "Please, just take care of her father."

Higgins tipped his hat, mounted and rode south toward the rise at an easy lope.

The two women turned to see Emma Creighton suddenly appear outside the front door of the ranch house. Emma waved angrily and shouted to the men at the corral.

Leslie slapped the lines on the buggy horse's rump, urging it off into a trot on the path that necessarily circled near the corral and barn on their left as they turned east.

As Emma waved and shouted from the front porch, the redheaded ranch hand jumped the corral fence and rushed, unarmed, to grab the right side of the harness and try to stop the horse. He called over Suellen's glare to Leslie.

"Sorry, ma'am, you're not supposed to leave the ranch."

Leslie snapped at him. "I have to see Miss Suellen home safely. Her father was just murdered."

"Please, ma'am," the cowhand pleaded, still clinging to the harness. "You'll get me in trouble."

"Get back!" Suellen warned, but he held onto the harness.

Suellen pulled her pistol, fired to hit near the hand's left boot just as the horse fought back on his hold. His boot moved so that her shot cut leather and stung his toes inside it.

He yelped, let go of the harness, and jumped back to hop around. "Yow!"

At the corral fence, sitting on the top rail, the freckled hand could not stop laughing. On the porch, a frantic Emma shook her fist at the men.

At the same time, on the ridge to the south, Higgins, having reappeared at the sound of the shot, found himself shaking with his own laughter.

Suellen drew back the hammer and aimed at the wounded hand's private parts.

The youth gasped in horror and backed away, still hopping around.

"Now get!" Suellen said to him.

The young hand danced back some more, then hopped toward the corral to sit on the edge of the trough to tug at his boot, while the other young cowhand continued to laugh.

Leslie drove on past the barn as Suellen holstered her pistol.

"You know, you are a bit scary." Leslie said, happily.

"He moved when I fired." Even in her grief, she found great satisfaction in fighting back, but turned to look around, toward the barn. "Will they follow?"

"Are you kidding?" Leslie asked with delight. "You scared that one half to death."

"Will you be okay when you get back here?"

"Yes, don't worry, but I'll wait with you until we know when the funeral is."

"Thank you," Suellen whispered. Once on their way, she let go of her tears and sobbed in her grief.

Watching from the ridge as they drove east over the rise and toward the flats, Higgins waited until he knew they were not being followed.

Satisfied, he turned south into the canyon.

Back in the red canyon near the hanging tree, Higgins returned to dismount and help Ben shift some of their gear to the backs of their saddles. They then put the blanket wrapped body on the pack horse and tied it in place.

Higgins rested a moment. "I saw your ma. She looks run down, but she sure is beautiful."

"She know who you are?"

"Not a chance."

Ben hesitated. "You see Lassiter?"

"No, just a couple of young cowhands."

Ben had become a fast gun for more than being a lawman. Someday he might face Lassiter. Everything was rolling toward some kind of deadly conclusion, an end that could take Ben's life. Yet he was here, and there was no turning back. He slowly paid attention to his friend's sudden story.

Higgins continued, amused. "And I sure got to tell you something funny. I stopped on the ridge to look back, and one young fellow tried to stop the buggy with your ma driving it and Suellen sitting beside her. So Suellen, she pulls a handgun and shoots him in the boot. He's hopping around like crazy, and then he tries again, so she aims a little higher, and he scatters. And the women drove off toward the east. Sure was funny."

Ben appreciated the story and was able to smile. Just for a second.

Higgins frowned. "Only other person I saw was a woman

outside the house, yelling to the hands. Maybe Creighton's wife."

Ben didn't respond, just listened.

"It was pretty obvious your ma was not supposed to leave the ranch." Higgins backed away from the pack horse. "From what I could gather, she was right miserable."

Ben knew that Higgins spoke the truth, and had deep regrets about having believed Lassiter's lies when he was a boy. He yearned to say he was sorry he could not have been big enough to help her.

"Do you think she knows my father is out of prison?" Ben asked.

"I ain't sure, but I figure she'd be real happy if she knew you was alive."

"I can't take that chance. She might give me away."

"Yeah, she might get real emotional."

"For now, I need to stay alive while I figure things out."

Higgins, his back to Ben as they gathered their mounts, didn't see the misery in Ben's face. "Your ma said there's a deputy in town, but I figure her uncle's money buys most everybody. So don't expect too much."

Ben nodded agreement.

* * * * *

While Ben and Higgins took the murdered sheriff toward town on the south road, and while Leslie drove Suellen home in the buggy, two men rode the Creighton range miles away to the north. They reined up on a rise overlooking rolling green hills with a distant herd of cattle representing only a fraction of the ranch's bounty.

Beyond the hills rose higher terrain with pines and black cliffs to the north. The land fell gently to the east as it spread toward the wide, open range. To the west, the snow crested Rocky Mountains towered over the lower hills where mining camps were known to be digging deep into a once pristine and beautiful rise of foothills.

Jed Creighton—in his sixties and bulky, polished, with crude features—looked kingly while hiding the inner torment with which he had lived since his wedding day. Wearing ranch clothes with a new Stetson and wearing a side arm, he put on a constant show of being in charge.

Harry Lassiter, in his forties, appeared slick and sleazy with a black mustache but handsome, dressed like a tin horn gambler in a slick blue vest. His easy manner hid his dislike of the rancher, his hand often on his holster as if for comfort.

Creighton leaned on the pommel, enjoying the view, despite his grim worries.

Lassiter managed a smile for the man who paid him well. "You do have it all. Mining shares, cattle, horses, and a spread taking up half the county."

"It was a long time coming."

But, Lassiter thought, *you never did anything right. Your big brother Ben told you not to marry Emma, and when you did, he left the ranch to Leslie. So you stole it from your own niece by getting her to sign a bunch of papers, and then you sold out and didn't pay her a penny. And that's how you bought this spread. Someday, I'm getting even, one way or another. And I know a way that will kill you without my firing a shot.*

Suddenly leery that Creighton could read his thoughts, Lassiter tried to look ready to do the rancher's bidding, as usual.

"Landry better not show up here," Creighton said. "Pardon or not, he murdered my kid brother. Shot him in the back."

"But your cousin in Texas, he said Boggs cleared Landry."

"Only casting doubt on how it happened. But I know darn well that Landry is guilty as sin. And he had Amos' money pouch in his saddle bags."

Lassiter nodded, thinking, *Yeah, and I know how it got there.*

Creighton, unaware of Lassiter's secret thoughts, sat staring at the distant herd with wrapped up in painful memories. His younger brother had been the innocent one in the family, a kid full of life and promise. That night Amos had gone to town to play cards and have fun, only to return to treachery in the barn. Creighton would never forgive Landry.

"So, has your cousin said anymore about the pardon?" Lassiter asked.

"No, I just got another letter, saying the governor fired him."

Lassiter adjusted his hat. "Well, it doesn't matter now. I figure twenty-five years in prison took the starch out of Landry. He may be down in Mexico with his tail between his legs."

"Yeah, and what if he finds out he had a son?"

"He won't. Everyone thinks the kid was mine. And besides, the little runt died a long time ago."

Creighton shrugged. "What'll Leslie do if she learns he's out?"

"Nothing. She belongs to me," Lassiter said.

They were silent awhile as the wind began to rise to a noisy whine. A red-tailed hawk sailed high above and zipped out of sight.

"I always thought the sheriff was one of us," Creighton said abruptly.

"He wore a badge too long to keep that up. I never did trust him, but anyhow, he won't be writing any more letters. The Hogans took good care of him."

"Yeah, but I only said to run him out of town."

"Zeke said it got out of hand when he put up a fight. Nobody planned it."

Creighton's thoughts were deep with regret. *How does a fight end up with a hanging*? After all these years, he knew there were few surprises left when Lassiter had a free hand. Sapped of moral strength the day he had married Emma, Creighton just rolled with the punches, year after year.

"Don't worry," Lassiter added. "Folks are too scared to speak up. It's just too bad the deacon got away from us."

"He's harmless," Creighton said.

Yeah, Lassiter silently mused, *but you never used to care, so you're maybe getting too darned old for this. I've been doing your dirty work for thirty years, just so you can give your wife whatever she wants. You're a beaten down wreck of a man, and you don't even know it.*

Creighton tugged at his hat brim. "Except now I'm worried about the sheriff's daughter."

"She doesn't know anything," Lassiter said. "I already checked with the deputy."

"No, I mean, I should buy her out, let her go back east."

"You feeling sorry for her?" Lassiter asked. "She has a nasty disposition."

"But she's just a girl."

"Yeah, a girl with a six shooter and a Yaqui backing her up."

Creighton looked amused. "You afraid of an Indian girl?"

"You haven't seen her throw a knife."

Creighton imagined every kind of way to see the gunman cut down like a dirty dog, and it would be satisfying for a woman to do it. He would forever regret allowing Lassiter to claim Leslie as his bride, even though the gunman treated her like a queen. With the passing years, Creighton had learned to fear and despise this man. Yet he was afraid to do anything about it, continuing to pay him to make things happen.

* * * * *

While Creighton and Lassiter were in the hills that same afternoon, Leslie drove the buggy with Suellen tearful at her side, moving east in the open on the north road. The palomino trailed on lead. The wind whipped up in gusts as clouds rose on the northern horizon.

With the shadow of the town in the far distance ahead, Leslie turned left and drove on a side road toward Suellen's single story house. Faded by wind and weather, the structure yet had a white picket fence around a struggling garden.

Beyond and to their left stood a stable and an empty corral. Green grass covered the field with the open range beyond.

Leslie drove up to the garden gate and stopped the buggy horse.

"Suellen, you can't stay out here all alone. Not now."

"Don't worry, I have Gina. When my father began spending his nights in town, he hired her to stay with me."

"Gina?"

"That's right, you never met her. She and her husband came up from Texas so he could work over in the mines, but he was killed in one of the shafts when it fell in last year. My father had met him, and since he had to leave me alone so often, he hired her to move in here and stay with me."

"But two women alone out here?"

Suellen managed a brief smile through her tears. "Don't worry. Gina's a full-blooded Yaqui Indian and she can throw a knife before half the men in town can draw. They're all afraid of her."

"Just the same, I'm not leaving until we know the time of the funeral," Suellen said. "And I want to see you lying down for awhile."

Out of the house came Gina, a pretty woman in a white blouse and dark skirt. At fifty, Gina—short and a bit chubby with long black hair tied back—seemed full of life. She wiped her hands on a towel.

Leslie and Suellen stepped down on the right side of the buggy.

"Gina, they hanged my father."

Leslie put her arm around Suellen to keep her from falling.

Gina, startled, turned angry as she took the palomino off lead and brought it around. "Go inside. I'll take care of the horses."

"Mrs. Lassiter will be here until we have word of the funeral." Suellen said and looked around. "Did my father's horse show up?"

Gina shook her head.

Leslie and Suellen retired to the house to rest.

SEVEN

As Ben and Higgins journeyed on the south road to town with the sheriff's body on their pack horse, and while Suellen and Leslie waited at Suellen's lonely place on the north road, the hands at the Creighton Ranch had a story to tell.

As Lassiter and Jed Creighton rode up to the corral, they saw the freckled ranch hand in the corral with the colts, but the redheaded hand cringed outside and seated on the trough's edge, his britches rolled up on his left leg to keep that foot in the water.

Lifting his left boot with a hole in the toe, the hand blurted out his story from the beginning to when he was shot.

"I tried to stop 'em, but that Miss Suellen, she shot me in the foot! My toes are so swollen, I can't never get my boot on." He now sputtered. "But I kept trying, only then she aimed at my privates and scared me silly."

Lassiter shifted in the saddle to look toward the house, hiding his grin.

Creighton struggled to keep a straight face. "Which way'd they go?"

The youth gestured east. "The north road. Ms. Leslie was taking her home on account of Miss Suellen was crying real bad. About her father being murdered or something."

Creighton and Harry Lassiter dismounted as the younger hand, freckles bouncing with his grin, came out to take their saddle horses. As the two men walked toward the house with their backs to the hands at the corral, they both grinned before sobering.

"Wish I'd seen that," Creighton said to Lassiter. "But who was the old man he was saying had hitched up the buggy?"

"I don't know. But my wife better get back here soon."

"She was just being kind to the girl."

"As long as she doesn't learn Landry's out."

As they entered the garden, over near the bench, they saw the folded newspaper.

Quickly, Creighton picked it up and opened to where the page had a torn item missing.

"She knows," Creighton said.

Inside the grand, well-furnished ranch house, Lassiter tipped his hat to Emma and then retreated to his rooms at the north end of the first floor, while Creighton remained in the parlor. He sat down in his big chair to gather his thoughts. He gazed around the plush room with its rosewood furniture and rich maroon drapery. He missed the old ranch house in Texas where he could pile up ropes or bring in a saddle.

Emma came to fuss over Creighton, leaning down to kiss his cheek.

She made it no secret that Leslie was an irritation. "That girl drove off like a crazy woman. He needs to punish her."

She helped him off with his boots as he leaned back.

"You don't get it, Emma," Creighton said. "He's crazy in love with her."

"But you paid him to marry her."

"He'd have done it for free." Creighton removed his hat and leaned further back, closing his eyes. He then placed his hat over his face.

"But now that Landry's out of prison, he'll want her back," Emma said.

"If he even shows up."

"If he does, what will you do about it?"

"That depends on Landry."

"But he murdered your brother!"

"Yeah, I know."

Emma, aware he was half asleep, spread a blanket over his legs and feet, then left the room as Creighton let his thoughts spin.

Creighton had to swallow every regret for the mistakes in his life. Yet, whenever he looked at Emma, touched her, enjoyed her kisses, he knew he could never escape her web. Every rotten thing he had ever done had been to make her happy.

He berated himself endlessly at having let himself become less of a man for giving in to her at every turn. Sleep finally came as a blessing.

* * * * *

Late that afternoon, Ben and Higgins, leading the burdened pack horse with a blanket covering the sheriff's body, rode east on the south road.

The distant cow town nestled on a flat on the south edge of a vast grassland that spread far north to green rolling hills, where cattle could be seen as dark specks. Beyond the free range, shadowy bluffs rose gray on the horizon.

"Creighton cattle?" Higgins questioned.

Ben didn't respond. Too much of the unknown lay ahead.

South of town to their right, the land stayed level only a short distance before it rolled down toward an eastbound creek, beyond which rose green, wooded hills with cottonwoods and dark shaggy pines, as far as the eye could see.

They passed the once-red livery barn on their right, where many horses moved around in the big corrals further back. They rode across a wide but rickety wooden bridge which spanned a low, wandering trickle leading south to the busier, wider creek. On their left stood a boarding house next to a cantina with music drifting out, soft but lively.

Only a few horses were at the rails. The boardwalks were rotting. The buildings needed paint. It looked as if no one really cared. A boarded-up newspaper office looked mostly forgotten among otherwise busy stores.

Not many men were about, and women were most likely home baking for the celebration. Two small boys darted out of the nearest alley with a little black dog, laughed in some secret game, and ran back out of sight with the dog trailing.

Decorations for the Fourth of July were everywhere with many flags waving in the breeze. Just past the two-story hotel was the barber's, and then the general store where boots and hats dangled from racks outside, while saddles rested on stands. Further on, steam rose from a Chinese laundry, and the aroma of hot bread came from the bakery near it. More stores and two saloons were further down.

"Now I'm hungry," Higgins muttered, sniffing the bread.

Further down on the left stood the sheriff's office and the jail, where a wagon blocked the front rails. Beyond, the undertaker sign could be seen, also on the left.

Far ahead at the end of the street beyond the buildings were the railroad corrals, still empty, and near a creaky, spinning windmill and several troughs. Across from the corrals, the chimney and ashes of what had been a church rested next to the cemetery on a knoll.

Men now gathered on the boardwalks to view the strangers with a body on their pack horse.

"Go on ahead," Ben said, exercising caution.

As Ben reined up near the hotel, Higgins and the pack horse continued to a space at the rail in front of the express office further along on the south side of the street, opposite the jail.

As Higgins dismounted, the deputy came out and crossed toward him.

A forty-year-old man, sloppy of build and garb, and needing a shave, with a rusty badge on his vest, Deputy Sheriff Porter could not be less friendly. His gun belt had a crooked holster as if he'd been sleeping with it. He lifted the blanket on the pack horse to uncover Sheriff Long's body as men gathered around.

Porter glared at Higgins. "You killed the sheriff?"

"That's the way we found him. In a canyon. Hanged."

"Maybe you'd better hand over your weapon. Right now." Porter backed away, tried to look threatening.

Just then Ben came walking over. His Deputy U.S. Marshal badge glittered in the sun, his twin holsters signaling trouble. Tall and husky, Ben had a commanding appearance.

Higgins gestured. "This here marshal can tell you we both came along at the same time."

Porter snorted. "Maybe you both done it." Then Porter met Ben's iron gaze. He backed off. It was obvious Porter was all bluff and no guts.

Two husky men came to help as Porter signaled to them. Higgins let the men lead the pack horse across the street and over to the undertaker's, where they could be seen lowering the body and talking to the skinny man in black.

One of the men led the pack horse back to Higgins. "Says he can set the funeral at eleven tomorrow morning. On Sunday."

"And his daughter?" Higgins asked.

"He said he'd send someone out to her place."

Then the man returned to help at the undertaker's. Onlookers had lost interest and most returned to where they'd come from, many of them heading further up the street to the saloons.

"Marshal," Higgins said, his back to Porter, "I'd admire to buy you some supper. After we find a place to bed down."

Ben nodded, ignoring the fidgety deputy. Higgins led his mount and the pack horse as they returned to where Ben had left his horse in front of the hotel.

Higgins muttered. "That deputy didn't show me much."

Leaving their horses at the rail, they entered the hotel with it's grand lobby and were immediately uncomfortable. They could see a restaurant further back. A staircase led to rooms upstairs.

When they stopped at the desk, the elderly clerk shook his head.

"Sorry, we're full up for the celebration, but the deacon, he's long gone, so you may be able to get his room over at the boarding house. Lady runs it says he was paid up to the Fourth, but don't look like he'll be back. Across the street, this side of the bridge."

Ben and Higgins paused, looking at the dining area with its white tablecloths.

The clerk grinned. "There's also a cantina over there with great Texas chili."

"Thanks," Higgins said.

After securing the deacon's room at the boarding house, Ben and Higgins delayed supper while they took their horses to the livery. The crusty, pint-sized livery man, Juggs, greeted them. His gray beard jutted outward.

"Saw you ride in," Juggs said. "Who were you packing?"

"The sheriff," Higgins said. "He was hanged."

Juggs frowned. "He was a good man. But don't expect much from the deputy. He blows with the wind, mostly from the Creighton Ranch."

Higgins agreed with a nod. "Can you take our horses?"

"You get my last two stalls up front," Juggs said. "Some fellahs didn't show up last night, so they're yours now. And there's room in one of the corrals out back for your pack horse."

"So, you'll be really busy tomorrow," Higgins suggested.

"Not so much," Juggs said. "They got the railroad corrals set up at the other end of town with feed and water. And some handlers. Creighton built it all up, figuring he'd hog the rail business, but it ain't here yet."

"I hear it's stuck in the Dakotas," Higgins said. "Who's Creighton?"

"Big he-bull with his own army and too many cattle." Juggs turned over the two stalls which were just inside the entrance of the barn.

"You fellahs going to do some of the shooting tomorrow? Rifles make good money as prizes. But never mind the fast-draw contest. Lassiter always wins."

Ben turned away to hide his dark, buried anger.

"Who's Lassiter?" Higgins asked.

"A hired gun, that's what. Married to Creighton's niece."

* * * * *

While Ben and Higgins put up their horses at the livery, a town handyman rode past on his way to the sheriff's home with news for Suellen.

After word was delivered and the man returned to town, Suellen stood on the porch of her house with Leslie, while Gina waited at the buggy.

"Thank you," Suellen said, her eyes red from crying.

Leslie, after giving Suellen a farewell hug for comfort, reluctantly walked over to her buggy where she climbed on board and took up the lines. She headed back to the Creighton Ranch late that afternoon, driving as slow as possible. She ached for her friend, and resented the terrible thing someone had done to be rid of the sheriff.

Realizing she was weak from the drive and all the excitement, she knew she would be back in bed before nightfall. Exhaustion still came over her from time to time.

As she drove back along the north road, a dark and cloudy sky soon turned the land gray and lifeless. That was how Leslie felt, as if her life would always be gloomy, lonely, and bitter with regret.

She knew her husband loved her and cherished her, but it

wasn't enough, not with Tom likely on his way north. She had a growing fear of great danger. Men had learned quickly not to even glance at her with Lassiter around. How would a forty-three-year-old man, just out of the confines of prison, even stand a chance of staying alive? Worse, someone who had once had his hands on Lassiter's wife?

Possessive and jealous, Lassiter would never abide Tom's presence. The thought terrified her.

She drove slowly over the rise and down toward the barns and corrals.

Lassiter greeted her at the buggy barn even as the freckled hand came to take over. Lassiter silently helped her down and walked at her side toward the house. Fearful of what he might say or do, she kept silent and tried to appear like she was not about to collapse.

"I was worried," he said, of a sudden.

Detecting no anger in his voice, she managed to speak up. "Suellen needed help. And the funeral is tomorrow at eleven."

"We're not going."

"But..." She paused to look at him, saw the dark in his gray eyes, the set of his jaw—as she had learned long ago, no argument was allowed.

"Your aunt and uncle will be there," he said. "And I need you to rest, so you can enjoy the Fourth."

He helped her up the stairs. Always attentive, he doted on her, loved her, and would never let anyone near her. Nor, she knew, would she ever be able to escape him.

As they entered the house, Lassiter saw Creighton asleep in his chair in the parlor, and no sign of Emma. As they turned right into a hallway leading to their quarters at the far end of the first floor, Suellen stopped, hand on the wall.

Then she folded, and Lassiter caught her up in his arms. Worried all the more, he carried her to their rooms.

* * * * *

That same evening, Higgins and Ben—overly stuffed by Mrs. Perez, the comely widow with flashing eyes—walked out of the cantina and into the twilight. They paused before heading for the livery to check on their horses and turning in at the boarding house.

"Mrs. Perez," Ben said with a grin, "she's got her eye on you."

"She's looking, all right, but I'm not the one."

"She's a widow with five kids, the waiter said."

"Not for me," Higgins denied.

Higgins had spent his life with the memory of his first love and child, both gone from him. Since, he preferred being alone, at least so far in his life. Yet he had to admit, there were times he started talking to himself, maybe a little too often.

They stood alone for now in the fading light.

Higgins turned to look to their right. "There's the deputy. And some mean looking fellahs."

Ben turned to follow his gaze. Further down the boardwalk, Deputy Porter and the three bearded, heavily-armed Hogan brothers were having a conversation.

"The Hogans," Ben said. "Got out of Deer Lodge a few months ago."

"So, that's them. They look like they ain't had a bath since."

"Probably not."

Immediately on seeing Ben, Zeke Hogan left the others and

came walking forward, hand on his holster. Ever known as the deadliest of the brothers, he dared Ben.

"Well, now, marshal, you're not so big without your shotgun."

Any second, there could be gunplay, but Porter quickly joined them and intervened, stepping forward and slightly ahead of Zeke, voicing a request for peace.

"Mr. Creighton don't want no trouble till after the Fourth."

"We can wait," Zeke said, his gaze searing.

As Zeke Hogan returned to join his brothers back down the boardwalk, Porter accosted Ben. "Why are you still here?"

"For the celebration," Higgins said.

"And," Ben nodded, "to investigate the hanging."

"You'll never find the vigilantes," Porter said.

"Who are they?"

Porter snickered. "Who knows?"

"And who pays them?"

"All the ranchers, but you won't never get 'em to say so."

Ben's gaze was red-hot. "And you're telling me the ranchers paid to hang a sheriff? Was he out branding mavericks?"

Porter, taken aback, had no answer and got huffy. "You'll live longer if you just leave town."

Porter turned to join and follow the Hogans down the street and over to a saloon, but before entering, he each turned to glare back at Ben. All bravado, Porter slapped his holster before strutting through the swinging doors and out of sight.

Higgins grunted. "That deputy's all hat and no guts."

"Not so the Hogans, though."

They turned and headed for the livery to check on their horses.

* * * * *

Sunday morning began with an overcast sky and a chilling wind. The funeral took place east of town at the cemetery, which set on a knoll near the remains of the burned down church with it's brick chimney still standing. An elder of the church, gray haired and in a black duster, read over the sheriff's grave.

Suellen wore a veil, and both she and Gina, who held her arm, had black capes.

Higgins, hat in hand, stood with the two women, but Ben held far back to the east side of the cemetery, where he had a good view of the visitors. He saw Jed and Emma Creighton, who put on a show with his Sunday suit and her expensive gown. He heard someone in the small crowd mention their names.

Jed Creighton, who had lost a brother named Amos down in Texas. That was all Ben had learned from bits of overheard conversation as a small boy. Only now, he was also aware Ben's real father had been the accused.

As a lawman, Ben had learned not to make assumptions nor to judge, but he knew that power and wealth could be a corrupting influence. He could see how the rancher had everyone catering to him even at a funeral, and how the man's wife had her nose in the air.

Only a few of the townspeople—all men—were present, including Deputy Porter. There was no sign of the three Hogans.

Ben thought grimly of Lassiter, who made no appearance, nor did Ben's mother. He felt relief there would be no confrontation during the ceremony. He knew how he'd feel if he saw the man who had brutalized his childhood, and that he must try not to let Lassiter figure out who he was, not just yet.

Ben felt unsure of what would come over him when he saw

his mother. It was unlikely she would recognize the six-foot, husky deputy as the skinny little boy she had lost.

No one knew Higgins, and he alone was aware of Ben's true identity.

With the ceremony over and as the crowd wandered off, Higgins spotted Boggs' marker with only a last name. He did not give himself away as the man's friend, but he mouthed a soft hello as he passed it.

Walking with Suellen and Gina, Higgins had a good look at the Creightons, who had held back, and he didn't like what he saw, but mostly because of Boggs' stories.

Seeing Ben watching on their right as they passed, Suellen stopped to snap at him. "Are you going to find the men who murdered my father? Or are you just going to stand around and look pretty?"

Ben, taken aback, stood speechless. He could only tip his hat.

Her words called everyone's attention to the glimmering badge with the circle star on his vest.

Suellen turned and addressed everyone as her voice rang loud and clear. "We'll be at the celebration tomorrow. And whoever did this had better not show up." At that moment, she drew her cape wide open to show her gun belt.

The darkening sky began to sprinkle with light rain drops.

Higgins tried to hustle her and Gina along but ran into the Creightons.

Creighton tipped his hat. "Miss Long, we had a great deal of respect for your father."

Suellen, chin up, glared at the rancher. "You're supposed to be the big he-bull around here, so how could you let this happen?"

Creighton, stunned at first, let out a startled laugh, then quickly sobered.

"How dare you make a mockery of it?" Suellen snapped at him, her hand on her gun belt as the cape moved further aside.

"Young woman," Emma said icily, "you've already shot one man. You should be in jail for that."

Higgins and Gina hurried Suellen away from them and toward the street, where their buggy awaited on the north side. Ben tipped his hat to Emma, ignored Creighton's curious gaze, and followed Higgins.

Jed Creighton's face had reddened, but Emma looked nasty.

The crowd dissipated in the lightly-falling rain, while the Creightons moved to the south side of the street under an eave, watching as Ben and Higgins assisted Suellen and Gina into their buggy.

Emma, still angered by Suellen, adjusted her bonnet and turned to her husband.

"She has no class. And that young marshal looks like trouble."

Creighton shrugged. "Lassiter will make sure he isn't."

"What would you do without Mr. Lassiter?"

"Maybe sleep better at night."

Emma studied him, then looked away.

They watched the women drive off, while Ben and Higgins walked on toward the cantina.

"Do you want to eat at the cantina for a change?" Creighton asked.

"No, the hotel dining room is a more respectable place."

But not as much fun, he wanted to say, turning as she took his arm.

* * * * *

Back at the Creighton Ranch after the funeral, rain still drizzled from a dark sky. Two older cowhands came to take the buggy at the garden gate where Jed and his wife stepped down.

Lassiter, standing on the porch out of the rain, tipped his hat to Emma as she walked ahead of Creighton and onto the porch.

She avoided his gaze and scurried inside. There was no sign of Leslie.

Jed Creighton stopped next to him, shaking rain from his hat. He paused to gaze around at this grand place, and wondered why. He had felt more at home on the beaten, weathered, old ranch. Suellen's angry words echoed in his ears, and he felt shame. He avoided his gunman's gaze for that reason.

"How was it?" Lassiter asked.

"The usual, but that Suellen is sure feisty."

"She's no worry."

"And there's a new kid lawman in town. Deputy U.S. Marshal. Porter said he's real nosy. Packs twin holsters. Looks like he knows how to use them."

Lassiter scoffed. "So?"

"If he doesn't leave, you need to help him do just that."

"We kill a federal marshal," Lassiter said, "it could bring trouble."

"He's a kid. Just scare him so bad he leaves." Creighton said, annoyed, and then changed the subject. "Where's your wife?"

"Asleep."

"Has the doctor been out?"

"No need, that's what he said. She just has to rest."

Lassiter led the way inside, as Creighton fretted, feeling crowded by everything and everyone.

* * * * *

After the funeral that Sunday afternoon, with drizzling rain smearing the windows, Ben and Higgins had hot chili in the crowded cantina. Off by themselves at a corner table, they watched diners come and go.

No one in the cantina put on airs. It seemed to always have a happy crowd with laughter and good food. An old Mexican with a gray beard sat off by the far wall, playing gentle tunes on his guitar. Patrons dropped money into his sombrero.

Mrs. Perez, the lonely but smiling widow, perky with a red ribbon in her black hair, brought them free cake and flirted with Higgins. He smiled, tipped his hat, and felt relief as she moved away.

"Long day," Higgins said, suddenly weary.

"I feel sorry for the girl," Ben said.

"Miss Suellen? Yeah, this was a sad day for her, but she's real tough, that one."

"I sure wouldn't want to cross her."

"She thinks you're pretty."

Ben gave him a grumpy look and didn't respond.

"Which makes me wonder why you ain't never found yourself a girl and got married."

"Too much trouble."

"Maybe so, but when Suellen came riding over the hill on that palomino and her yellow hair was blowing in the wind, you were thunderstruck."

"Liking what you see and getting your feet wet are two different things." Ben's denial sounded right, but inside, he knew that his first sight of her had thrown him for such a loop, he couldn't get her image out of his thoughts—or his dreams.

They finished their chili as Mrs. Perez, twinkling, brought them coffee and apple pie on the house, then left them alone. Higgins had the largest slice, which was no surprise.

Higgins savored the coffee and enjoyed the pie. "I reckon about now, Creighton's telling Lassiter about the new lawman in town."

"I don't know what I'll do when I run into him."

"Lassiter?" Higgins made a face. "I'll tell you what you'll do. Nothing. He won't know who you are. No one will. Except if your ma sees you face-on, watch out. Mothers have an uncanny way of knowing their own kids, no matter how much they've grown."

"She could give me away."

"Come tomorrow, you just don't go around the fancy folks where she'll be sitting. Keep in the crowd, as cover." Higgins downed his coffee. "Juggs, over at the livery, he said the gun shooting contests are off by a creek, away from the big doings. And how Lassiter only enters for the fast draw and always wins."

"Sure would like to take him down a peg or two."

Higgins shrugged. "And if you don't?"

"I'll at least worry him some." Ben leaned back. "But I'd sure like to get some answers before my real pa gets here."

"Well, that'll be weeks, most likely." Higgins shrugged. "But prison takes a lot out of a man. He may never show."

"Then I'll have to go on down to Texas."

They both fell silent. Higgins had on his mind to try to keep Ben out of trouble.

Ben's thoughts were on a father he never knew. Guilty or not, at least he wasn't Lassiter.

His father could be short or tall, skinny or hefty. He could have relatives all over, or he could have no one. Maybe he loved Ben's mother. Maybe not. After twenty-five years in prison, he could be nasty and explosive. Or he could be a beaten wreck of a man.

But, again, at least he wasn't Lassiter.

EIGHT

While Ben and Higgins lingered over their coffee at the cantina Sunday afternoon, excitement was about to greet Tom Landry and Matlock along the south road as they headed toward Hang Town. The pack mule trailed them.

With an overcast sky and light drizzle, they rode in silence with the town still just a shadow far ahead of them. They could barely make out the shape of the livery barn up front and where the north and south roads came together at a bridge. They could see the same distant wooded hills that had been in view to their right for some time.

Matlock only thought of being there to take care of Ben.

Tom Landry, unaware he had a son, wondered what it would be like to see Leslie after twenty-five years. He would know her anywhere, but he doubted she would see the same kid in this aging, bearded man, just out of prison. He wasn't sure if he could handle her being with a husband, let alone a hired gun.

Startled by a thunderous noise from the right, they reined up.

A bay horse came galloping up from the south across the grassland, closer and closer with head tossing and kicking wildly. A saddle dangled halfway down the left side of its belly. With reins flying, it looked too dangerous to catch. It crossed the road in front of them and continued north. It bucked off and on and broke from a gallop to a weary trot.

"He's gonna hurt himself," Matlock said, freeing his lasso and turning his mount.

The two men set out at a lope, chasing the bay as it quickly crossed the north road and headed up a path toward a small ranch. It aimed for the barn, but the saddle dropped under its belly, and the frightened horse set about bucking crazily before it even passed the house.

In the corral, Suellen's palomino mare danced about in panic.

As the bay spun in front of the house, kicking up dirt and flowers, Gina dashed outside. Wearing a white blouse and whirling dark skirt, her long black hair flying, she was a startling and beautiful sight.

The two men reined up in surprise as she rushed close to the bay and tried to grab the reins, but she was knocked back, falling on her rear.

Tom Landry dismounted. "Ma'am, let us handle it."

Once again, Gina got up and tried to grab the reins. The bay hit her hard as it spun, putting her back on the ground on her backside.

Matlock, who had his lasso ready with a loop, threw fast and sure from the saddle. The catch fell around the bay's neck and held.

At that point, the latigo broke and the saddle hit the dirt under the bay's legs, making it buck all the more. Matlock took a dally around the horn and backed his mount until the bay spun and stopped bucking. Free of the saddle, it stood shuddering.

Tom moved in cautiously on foot. He caught the reins and bravely put a soothing hand on the bay's neck. It trembled but accepted the sudden comfort, strangely held in check by Tom's low voice.

Matlock freed the dally, and Tom took control of the rope, while still stroking the frightened animal. The bay warmed to Tom and nosed him as he whispered to it.

Exhausted and still seated on the ground, Gina started to rise.

Matlock jumped down, startling her. He picked her up in his big arms with her skirts swirling about her feet. She kicked air and squirmed, hitting at him.

"Put me down, you big oaf!"

Matlock laughed, bounced her up and down, and then set her on her feet. She shoved him away.

From under her skirts, she pulled a long hunting knife and threatened him.

Startled, Matlock tried to back away, tripped on his own boot, and fell back. He landed flat on his rear with a loud grunt.

Gina drew up to her full height, staring at the silly look on Matlock's face. She laughed and secured her knife under her skirts. She had never seen such a lovable-looking buffoon.

Matlock finally grinned and stumbled to his feet. His hat had fallen back on the chin strap, but he drew it on, then tipped it at her forced scowl. He caught up his horse, along with Tom's, and the lead to the pack mule.

Tom Landry had the bay calm and steady now. He turned to Gina. "Yours?"

Gina shook her head. "The sheriff's. Sheriff Long. He was hanged by vigilantes."

Startled, Tom felt shame and hurt. He didn't know for sure why the sheriff had been hanged, but it cut like a knife to think he might be the reason. It was the man's letter that had led to Tom's pardon. Humbled, he fought for breath. His heart pained him.

Gina sensed Tom's strange reaction. "The funeral was this morning. His daughter's asleep in the house."

Matlock sobered. "Why'd they hang a lawman?"

Gina shrugged. "This is Hang Town, that's why."

Tom, badly shaken, led the sheriff's horse to the corral where he turned it loose inside. It headed for the barn while the palomino danced around. Tom hung the bridle on the gate post.

Returning to pick up the saddle, Tom turned to Gina. "You want us to give it a rubdown?"

"No, I'll do it. You go on to town before it rains any harder," she said. "I can't ask you in because Miss Suellen needs to rest up for tomorrow."

"She's going to the celebration?" Tom asked, surprised.

"She wants to see who looks guilty."

Tom took the saddle and blanket to the corral and set it on the top board.

Returning, Tom mounted and tipped his hat. He had to swallow his grief for the man who may have risked his life to set Tom free. He felt beaten, shattered. He could only pray he was not to blame.

Matlock, mounted with the mule's lead in hand, was reluctant to leave as he touched his hat brim. "Ma'am, I'd sure like to give you a whirl on the dance floor tomorrow."

She didn't answer, but her eyes were twinkling.

Matlock grinned and rode away with Tom, but he kept looking back until she went to the barn. The big man had never felt so in love, or so he told himself. Gina had looked so cute and feisty, he had lost complete control of his senses and felt unbridled joy. He knew she could fill his life with wonder. It never occurred to him that it might be otherwise.

Tom, riding just ahead, struggled with his own emotions, painful and full of remorse. From the day a couple of teenagers had eloped some twenty-five years ago, a chain of unthinkable events had followed, perhaps leading to the death of an honorable, courageous sheriff. This was Creighton country, and the sheriff had freed a man whom Creighton had sworn was guilty of murdering his kid brother. There was no way not to see a connection.

Nothing Tom could do would change what had already happened, and he couldn't turn back. He needed answers, and God help him, he wanted to see Leslie one more time.

* * * * *

Late Sunday in light rain, Tom and Matlock, pack mule trailing, rode up to the livery, short of the bridge over the trickling creek, and in sight of the bustling cow town as the town's people worked to get everything ready for the Fourth. Lamps could be seen as twilight fell.

They rode into the wide open doors of the livery barn where they reined up in the light of several lamps hung on posts. It looked like the stalls were all taken.

Juggs, the wiry little old man with the jutting gray beard, came out of nowhere.

"Looks like you're full up," Tom said.

Juggs stopped cold, saw the Texas saddle. "Say that again?"

Tom shrugged. "We need a place for our horses. And if you're of a mind, we can pay to sleep in the loft."

"A Texan!" Juggs chirped happily. "A voice from home! Set yourselves down. I got bunks in my tack room out back, and there's a little corral with a shed I always save. And hot stew on the stove in my house."

Tom and Matlock happily accepted and dismounted.

Juggs looked at Matlock's size and grinned. "Yeah, I got enough for you, too."

Matlock, leading his mount and the mule, just chuckled.

Tom wearily led his horse behind them toward the back entrance. He had come a far piece, and confrontations would soon be inevitable. He knew of Creighton's hired gun, Lassiter. He knew there could be trouble. But there was no turning back.

Later that night when Ben and Higgins checked on their horses in the forward stalls, they were unaware of Juggs and his visitors just behind the barn.

Ben had his own thoughts, his own drive for answers. Tomorrow on the Fourth of July, maybe, just maybe, he would learn more about his real father before Landry ever arrived in Hang Town. Maybe he could force himself to look at Lassiter without slapping leather in anger. Perhaps he could see his mother's lovely face without having tears in his eyes.

And if he was lucky, he could beat Lassiter at the contest.

Higgins, meanwhile, only thought of protecting Ben.

* * * * *

Early Monday morning on a now sunny day at the celebration for the Fourth of July, the grounds behind the hotel bustled with activity. Shaded by tarps on poles, tables were alive with food and drink preparations, set just south of the hotel, not far from the wood dance floor, which had no cover of its own, and set further east of the tables.

A tent with closed flap stood alone between the dance floor and the hotel, it's sign reading: JUDGE'S TENT. Further away from the dance floor, many tarps and tents were set up with chairs and benches in preparation for possible rain, or to avoid the hot sun.

South of the food tables and down the green, grassy slope to the distant, busy creek, preparations for the shooting contests were ongoing. Beyond the stream and before Douglas firs, bunchy junipers, and dwarf maples crowded the slopes, rifle targets stood in a clearing. Boxes of bottles were set aside for the fast-draw contest near the creek but behind a high wall of wood to protect the innocent celebrants up the hill from any wild shots.

Behind the livery barn that same Monday morning, Matlock and Tom lingered over their coffee in Juggs small house, until Juggs got lively about the sweet treats they would soon find at the celebration. They downed their coffee and readied to return to the livery.

Meanwhile, Ben and Higgins had checked on their mounts in the forward stalls and then walked back to the wide entrance, stopping just inside. They were shadowed and not readily seen as they watched the buggies and riders moving east toward the hotel. They could hear the distant music and some laughter to their right.

They held back in the shade because the bright sun rising from the east was blinding. For a moment, they twisted about to see Juggs talking to unseen persons outside the back door, a far distance away in the big, long barn. They lost interest and turned their gaze back to the busy street and growing noise from behind the hotel further east.

They watched buggies and riders coming in from the west with the bright morning sun in their eyes. All of a sudden, the sound of firecrackers popped up the street to their right just over the bridge, startling riders and teams. A dozen children were shouting in the street beyond.

Ben and Higgins were unaware of Tom entering the barn's rear door far behind them. Leaving Matlock to dawdle with Juggs outside the back entrance, Tom's forward stroll was not heard over the outside clatter. Tom stopped some distance behind Ben and Higgins, who were strangers to him, but he remained within earshot as he checked a saddle for sale on a rack to his left.

Up front, Ben and Higgins saw Lassiter's buggy coming into view from the west. They backed further into the dark of the livery where they were not easily seen because of the bright morning sunlight.

Tom was still unnoticed, as Ben and Higgins both turned grim.

With the sun in his eyes, Lassiter drew his hat down and pulled his buggy horse to a brief halt directly in front of the barn entrance, waiting for the street to clear. As he grimaced with impatience, Leslie used her hand to shade her eyes, but it was so bright she looked down and drew her blanket around her. Neither one saw the men inside the livery in the shadows.

Seeing Lassiter, Ben's boyhood fury returned, but looking at his mother, his heart swelled with forgotten love in his chest.

Higgins gestured, nodded to Ben. "There's Lassiter, and your ma."

Behind them, Tom caught his breath. *What*? He left the saddle and moved a bit closer, still unnoticed, so he could see past them to the street. At first he only saw the nasty looking man who had to be Lassiter, sitting stiff and holding the lines. Then suddenly, Lassiter leaned down to look at the traces. Tom saw Leslie, still beautiful, and twenty-five years melted away. *My God.*

Lassiter cracked his whip and drove forward over the bridge, scattering the kids.

Higgins turned to Ben. "She'd sure be happy to know you're still alive."

Ben could only nod. Badly shaken at the sight of the man who had terrorized him when he was a boy and who was still known as the fastest draw west of the Mississippi, he yet felt a yearning at the sight of his mother for the first time in twelve years. Seeing her looking frail and vulnerable, he hated himself for ever thinking she could have physically or otherwise prevented her husband's cruelty, had she even suspected.

Behind Ben and Higgins, Tom felt his knees about to cave. He sidestepped left to put his hand on a stall frame. With the buggy out of sight, he backed further and further away, not wanting them to notice him or wonder if he had heard.

The street grew quieter with children being herded to the festival and fire crackers confiscated temporarily. Buggies and riders continued in from the west, everyone shading their eyes.

At that moment, Ben and Higgins heard Matlock's laughter as he and Juggs came forward into the livery from the back door. Tom still held onto the stall frame.

Ben and Higgins turned but were unaware Tom had heard them.

At the same time, Tom saw Ben's face and his circle star. This tall young man was Leslie's son? Why would she be surprised to find her son alive? And why didn't they refer to Lassiter as the father? Tom was at his wits' end.

Ben saw the stranger and liked his appearance, but still had no clue.

Matlock hurried forward, past Tom, to grab Ben's hand. "Hey, marshal, I come all this way to take care of you."

Higgins nodded with a chuckle. "Somebody has to."

Ben gestured. "My friend Higgins. Mr. Matlock."

Matlock shook Higgins' hand, crushing it so Higgins winced.

Higgins finally grinned, but didn't call to anyone's attention Matlock's wild spree in Gorman's Creek.

Matlock turned and grabbed Tom's left arm, bringing him a few steps closer. "This is my friend, Texas."

"Texas?" Higgins questioned.

"Yeah," Matlock added, "but he just spent a year in an army hospital in the Dakotas. I'm going to show him the doings so we can fill our bellies and put some fat on him."

Tom slowly met Ben's gaze as Ben offered his hand. When Tom gripped the lawman's strong hand, he nearly collapsed. Why did the kid look so familiar?

At the same time, Ben had funny sensations as he drew back.

Higgins also held out his hand to Tom, who took it. "My name's Higgins, and the kid here is Ben Cross."

Tom drew a deep breath. "So where you from, marshal?"

Higgins quickly answered. "He's from Montana. I'm up from Colorado. We met on our way here."

Ben sensed Higgins' caution. Not every one from Texas where the Creightons had ruled was necessarily a friend. From what he had often overheard from Lassiter, his mother's Uncle Jed had his hand in everyone's pocket in West Texas and had ruled every inch of it. He tried to concentrate on Matlock's jolly nature instead of the past.

"Yeah," Juggs said to Tom and Matlock. "These fellahs found the sheriff hanging up in some canyon."

Matlock made a face. "We found his horse running loose."

"Yeah," Juggs said. "Sheriff Long. Left a daughter."

Now Tom felt again the pain of knowing a lawman may have paid a price for setting him free. He had no way of thanking the man, except within his nightly prayers.

Matlock adjusted his hat and preened a bit. "Yeah, his horse was bucking with a saddle under it's belly, but Texas here, he just whispered in its ear, and it just sort of fell in love with him. Like I did with that pretty little, black-haired gal living there. And she's got a real big knife."

Juggs chuckled. "That's Gina. Full blooded Yaqui."

Matlock grinned. "Yeah? I can handle her, you wait and see."

Juggs burst out laughing. "You're kidding, right?"

With Ben reeling from seeing his mother and Lassiter, and Matlock jawing about Gina, no one saw how sick Tom looked until he reeled back against the stall and held on.

"Hey, Texas" Juggs said to Tom, "you ain't saying you're sick from my flapjacks?"

Matlock helped Tom over to a stool where he could sit down. "No, he maybe just got out of that hospital a little too soon. What got you, Texas? Sioux or Cheyenne?"

Tom flushed, embellishing his story. "Ambush in the Black Hills. Never saw what hit us."

Ben was overly curious about Tom, yet turned to the street to watch as the Creightons passed into view. Jed drove the buggy in his Sunday suit while stiff and proper Emma sat at his side in her laced finery and feathered bonnet. Tom could see past Ben with painful recollection.

Juggs gestured. "Them's the Creightons."

Yeah, Tom said to himself. *I remember him holding the noose.*

"Well," Higgins suggested, "maybe it's time we moseyed over to where they got all that grub."

"I'll catch up with you fellahs," Juggs said. "Got to finish watering out back."

Juggs returned to the back entrance and disappeared outside.

Matlock took charge of Ben and walked in the lead with him out in the sunlight, while Tom, seemingly recovered, brought up the rear with Higgins. They all pulled their hat brims down as much as they could to dodge the glare of the sun.

Moving east along the south boardwalk with a crowd ahead of them, Tom spoke quietly to Higgins. "That marshal, he sure seems young for the job. How old do you figure he is?"

Higgins, ever alert, shook his head. "Got no idea."

Silent now, Tom stewed over what he had heard. 'Lassiter, and your ma.' Higgins had not said, 'your ma and pa.'

Meanwhile, Higgins had no idea that Tom was the expected ex-convict, because in Higgins' mind, it was many weeks too soon. That made the Texan mighty suspect and dangerous with his questions. Higgins always remembered the skinny little kid he had been unable to protect. Now, no one was going to back-shoot his young friend. Not if Higgins could help it.

Tom, however, was chomping at the bit to learn more.

Matlock and Ben led the way, turning right through the busy alley west of the hotel and moving out in back where many flags waved from poles. Sack races were already creating laughter, horseshoes were flying, tug-of-wars were spilling folks, and kids were running in circles, all west of the food.

Shaded by tarps, tables were heavy with cakes, cookies, and hot dishes with heaps of bread, and hungry townsfolk filling their plates. Women in aprons were already serving the hungry. Between the feast and the hotel's back entrance, tables also held hand-sewn clothing, pottery, canned jams and jellies, baskets, and fine linens for sale.

Flags and banners were everywhere with red, white, and blue streamers.

Matlock was first to the food, with Ben, Higgins, and Tom following close behind.

Three fiddlers were setting up on the dance floor.

Some distance east of the dance floor with a view of the festivities, some ten large tarps were on poles to shade from the sun. One grand tarp spread over chairs in a row with a view of the games, dance floor, and food, was reserved for the Creighton Ranch and set furthest south, just at the top of the slope that led down to the creek.

Not easily seen by the crowd, Leslie—her coat off to show

her pretty print dress—and Lassiter were there at the reserved tent. He sat her in the front row with a view of the crowded festivities but not of the contest area at the creek. He gave her a kiss on the cheek and a glass of lemonade, then left her alone as he headed back to talk with Jed Creighton near the hotel's back porch.

Meanwhile at the tables, Emma wore her tailored outfit and Paris bonnet as she lorded it over the ladies of the other ranches, farms, and town. They tolerated her because Creighton's wealth touched everyone's livelihood. She didn't see the sour faces often secretly appearing when her back was turned.

Unseen by Leslie because of the crowd and food tarps, Ben and Higgins sat at benches with Matlock and Tom, furthest away from the dance floor. They could see Creighton and Lassiter at the back of the hotel, seemingly engaged in serious conversation and also unaware of the four strangers observing.

Watching Lassiter, Ben had trouble eating. He washed it down with strong coffee.

Children danced around near Matlock, who sat at the end of the table. They were singing "Yankee Doodle Dandy" and whirling around. With a grin, the big man took out his harmonica and got up to play the tune.

Delighted, the girls and boys, five each, clasped hands and danced circles around him as he hopped and played. He was surprisingly light on his feet. Nearby members of the crowd watched with delight.

Beyond by the dance floor where the fiddlers were tuning up, Gina—wearing a red shawl over her colorful dress—paused to step up on the wooden platform to look far over the crowd at Matlock playing and dancing with boys and girls, who circled him. It was a pleasing sight.

Suellen, who wore a black jacket over dark skirts, joined her.

"What a big dopey guy," Gina said, trying to stay detached.

"But he's kind of cute," Suellen prodded.

They watched until Matlock plopped back down at the food table. The children tried to get him up again, but he wouldn't budge, exhausted. Some people at the table were now standing, blocking their view of all but his hat.

From where she stood with Suellen, Gina giggled. "He's a goof ball."

Suellen enjoyed the moment, then they both sobered as they stepped down and walked their way over to the far tent at the edge of the slope to see Leslie, still alone under the big tarp. Food and mugs of coffee had now been placed inside on a table near her and within reach.

As Leslie smiled up at them, Gina pointed to the far side of the slope as big Matlock and bearded Tom, hats shading their faces, were walking down toward the creek among a crowd of men.

"That's Matlock, the big guy, the grizzly," Gina said to Leslie. "Him and that old bearded guy, they took care of the sheriff's horse."

Unable to see all of Tom's face, Leslie yet felt a funny spin to her insides, and when he suddenly turned his head just long enough for her to see his features, her stomach reeled. "Who is that man, the one with the beard?"

"I don't know," Gina said. "But he was very nice."

Leslie, in turmoil, struggled with disbelief.

"Can we bring you something?" Suellen asked her. "Some pie?"

"No, thank you, maybe later."

Gina and Suellen worried over how pale Leslie suddenly looked, but wondered off toward the food tents.

Leslie smiled after them, but then she frowned. She leaned from her chair, twisting to see past the poles, trying to get a glimpse of the crowd as it left her field of vision on its way to the creek. She could no longer see the bearded stranger. She turned back to her view of the tables and dance floor and shook her head.

Not possible, she told herself.

Knowing Tom could not arrive for another month, but hoping he would never come north for his own sake, Leslie found herself thinking back to what had started out with such love, and ended so badly. It didn't matter because she was lost to him now.

She was not only married and had recently suffered another failed pregnancy that left her weak as a kitten, but her husband was also a dangerous man. She closed her eyes to stifle her tears.

Ben and Higgins, unseen by Leslie, stood in the middle of dozens of men around the food tables, intending to join the crowd moving down the slope toward the creek. They stopped just past the tables as Suellen, alone now, approached them.

Higgins tipped his hat as did Ben.

"I'm so sorry about the way I acted," she said to both of them. "I'm grateful you took care of my father."

Higgins nodded. "Anything we can do for you now?"

"Just find out who did it and why."

Higgins and Ben could only nod, and she zeroed in on Ben.

"Please, if you are in the fast-draw contest, don't let Lassiter win."

"Won't be easy," Higgins said.

She and Ben gazed at each other a long moment, and to herself, she concluded, *he has the bluest eyes.*

Ben in turn felt overwhelmed by her. Being close to someone so beautiful and real, with such warmth and sass, was just a little more than he could handle.

Then she smiled at him. "I am sorry I said those mean things to you, Marshal."

"Enough to dance with him?" Higgins asked her with a grin. "You did say he was pretty."

Embarrassed, she flushed. "I'm not dancing," she said, touching her dark clothes, reminding them she was in mourning.

She gave them a small smile as they tipped their hats again, and moved on down into the middle of the growing crowd of men, anxious to see the contests. She turned to glance back over her shoulder more than once.

Unaware of her watching them, Ben muttered to Higgins. "I can't dance."

"Sure you can. Just walk around and hop now and then."

Over in her tent, Leslie was frustrated because she had no view of the creek unless she stood up and walked forward a long distance. Knowing her husband would stop her from leaving the shade, she could only fuss and fret.

Not having had a glimpse of Ben and Higgins, she thought only of the man with the beard, the stranger.

She tensed as Lassiter returned to see if she was content.

"I can't see the creek," she said.

"But I want you to stay here."

She hedged. "I won't see you win the contest."

"They built a wall, to protect everyone from stray shots, and you can't see it from this side of the hill anyway. But I'm going to win that silver saddle before the day is over. Just wish me luck."

"Good luck then."

Lassiter, who only counted on his skill and never luck, looked as if he had already won. He bent over to kiss her cheek and left her.

Still wondering about the bearded man, she kept telling herself that Tom could not possibly arrive for several more weeks. It was unlikely, even then, she would recognize him after so many long years.

NINE

As Ben, Higgins, Tom, and Matlock mingled with the crowd down at the creek, they viewed the sign spelling out the shooting contests. It hung on a wooden wall that was some eight feet wide and almost as tall and read:

ENTRY FEE, SIX BITS EACH CONTEST

RIFLES 2 P. M.
Prizes: Five Silver Dollars, Each Win.

No Buffalo Guns.

FAST DRAW 4 P. M.
Single action only.

ONE GRAND PRIZE, SILVER SADDLE.
See it in the Judge's Tent.

All of a sudden, lively music from the dance floor came echoing down with such volume, Matlock turned to his friends. "I got to find that little gal and dance with her before some other galoot beats me to it."

They grinned as the big man hurried on his way back up the

slope to find Gina. Up by the handicraft tables with Suellen, Gina looked up at the joyful Matlock, who bowed, then offered his hand.

"That's our dance," he said.

"You big oaf, you'll step on my feet."

"No, little lady. Your feet won't touch the floor."

Gina had to laugh at his bravado and yielded.

Suellen moved around to sit next to other women on the benches near the wooden floor. She watched with envy as Matlock escorted Gina to middle of it. Deputy Sheriff Porter also was watching from the food tables.

Matlock swung Gina about, often with her feet not touching the floor. She had to laugh at the very joy in his face and manner.

After a lot of hot-stepping and twirling, Matlock and Gina stopped as the music ended. Matlock held her hand, bent way down to kiss it, and straightened. It made her feel as silly as he was.

Porter came up to them. "I'm cutting in."

"Not unless you grow a lot bigger than you are," Matlock said.

Porter, staring up at the big man, then looked to Gina for help and got none.

"You'll be sorry," Porter said to Matlock.

"Yeah, I'm crying already," Matlock said with a chuckle.

Porter stomped off, muttering to himself.

The music started again, and as Matlock swung Gina about, she looked up at him with a giggle. "Why are you such a fool?"

"I'm only a fool about one thing, and that's you, little gal."

He swung her off the floor and spun her around again.

* * *

Down at the creek, rifle shooting was imminent with targets set far off in the distant cottonwoods and dark pines. Crusty buffalo hunters, ranch hands, young hot shots, local men, all prepped for the contest, waded across the shallow but busy stream where they would set up at the rifle stands.

Ben, standing with Higgins, watched for Lassiter, but he assumed the gunman would not show until the fast draw, which was two hours away. He knew it would be painful to even be close to the man, but he was not a skinny little kid anymore. He also had a fair chance of winning and putting Lassiter in his place. It would not erase tortured memories, but it would sure feel good, even if just for a moment.

Tom also had a lot on his mind, saw children to his left and further east up the creek, poking at skeeters while searching for pollywogs. He started slowly toward them, walking alone, his back to the contest crowd.

Tom shook his head, deep in thought. First, there was the daughter of the sheriff who had sent the letter that set Tom free. It might never be known if Tom's freedom had cost the lawman his life, but the question weighed heavy on Tom's mind.

He stopped near the laughing children and looked back to where Higgins and Ben were enjoying the pending rifle shoot among the growing crowd of men. He didn't know if he could possibly be that young lawman's father, but if he was, it would sure be a source of much-needed pride.

Now he was about to face a terrible trauma, the moment he would try to let Leslie know he was here. She was the only one who might shed light on the past.

Tom looked around and up the slope where the makeshift tents rested on the crest of it. The first tent was Creighton's. He saw Leslie from her waist down where she sat in a chair. At the moment, it appeared she was alone. She could not see him from where she sat facing the dance floor and shaded tables.

The crowd covered the northwestern half of the slope with fun and games. Many were dancing and some were still feasting. He looked back down at the rifle contest and no one paid him heed. Bravely, Tom circled further and then walked up the rise unnoticed by anyone. He moved up behind the tarp.

Beyond the creek and far back in the woods, rifle fire had started.

He knew his presence would shock her, but he had to learn what Leslie knew of the reasons he was arrested. And he had to ask if he had a son, without putting Ben in danger.

At the same time, he tried not to think about her being another man's wife. He told himself enough time had passed that he could handle it. Sweat on his forehead and back said otherwise.

He came to a halt on the south side of the tarp. All that could be seen from inside were his legs from the knees down, but she was still unaware of his presence. Tom looked carefully around and back down to the creek and contest. He was in the clear, but his knees were shaking.

Not minding that she was alone, Leslie wearily sipped her lemonade. Until a deep voice with a strong Texas drawl spoke behind her.

"Leslie, please don't turn around."

She panicked, her hand to her breast, didn't turn. "Tom?"

"Yes."

Leslie could barely get her breath. His voice was deeper, but she knew it was him. It all came back as real as life itself. The runaway romance with a skinny teenager, their wedding, the nights on the prairie before they were tracked down. She thought she had put it behind her years ago, but now it closed in around her. She stammered in reply.

"I saw you walking down to the creek, but I didn't believe it possible." She fought the urge to turn. "I'm so glad you're free, but how?"

"Sheriff Long sent a letter."

"Dear God, Suellen's father." She choked on her sudden sob.

"Was that why he was hanged?"

"I don't know," she responded. "But no one here expects you for several weeks."

For a long moment, they were silent as her tears came. Tom knew he might only have a minute of privacy with her and jumped to the big question.

"I have to know, did we have a son?"

Leslie gasped in surprise, wiped at her tears. "Oh, Tom, I'm so sorry, yes, and that's why I had to get married right away, but he died when he was twelve."

Tom hesitated, remembering what was said about her being Ben's mother. He chose not to torture her until he was sure. "How did it happen?"

She sobbed. "He ran way from home and drowned in the river."

Tom swallowed the news. "Why did he run away?"

"I don't know. My husband said he stole money from us and was afraid of being caught and punished."

"You believed him?"

"Tom, you don't understand. I've never had a choice."

He held back as he knew she was suffering. It seemed everyone had lied to her most of her life, and she had no way to prove otherwise.

"But Tom, you're not safe here." She turned to see Emma looking toward her. "My aunt's watching me. Please stay away from me, for your own sake."

"That will never happen."

"Tom, please…"

There was a long silence as she waited. And waited.

"Tom?"

No answer, so she bravely turned in her chair. There was no sign of him.

Back down at the creek, unseen by anyone above, Tom paused to pull himself together. He took a moment alone by the busy water. "I just spent twenty-five years in prison. I'm not wasting any more time. I've got to find out."

While Matlock whirled Gina on the dance floor among the crowd of swingers, Deputy Sheriff Porter watched with Creighton and Lassiter from where they stood on the back porch of the hotel.

Porter wet his lips. "I'd sure like to get my hands on that Gina."

Creighton shook his head with a grin. "You can't tame a Yaqui. Too blamed independent. They'll fight at the drop of a hat."

Porter would not be deterred. "I heard they were farmers."

"And hunters," Creighton said, "and the Jesuits had a big influence before the trouble started. Then Mexico learned it was like trying to tame a bobcat. So did any stray Texan if he ran afoul of one."

"If they all look like her," Porter said, "it'd be worth it."

Porter glared at Gina and Matlock on the wooden platform as they out-danced everyone else with the lively music. Irritated, Porter walked down the steps and back toward the food.

"He's got it bad," Lassiter said with a sneer.

Creighton nodded. The older he got, the more amused he was at what drove other men to distraction.

Lassiter preened. "Did you see that silver saddle in the judge's tent? I'm going to win it."

"I'll buy it from you," Creighton offered.

"No, I'm keeping it."

They paused to listen to the lively music. They both knew Leslie was not well enough even for a slow tune. They also knew Emma would never dignify that wild dance floor with her presence.

Creighton adjusted his hat. "I have to walk out quite a ways to have a good view of the fast draw. You think you have any competition?"

"No matter. I never lose."

They could hear the rifle fire in the beginning rounds.

Creighton secretly hoped someone would beat the arrogant gunman.

Lassiter stayed with his boss, not interested in going down to the creek until it was show-off time.

Over on the dance floor, Matlock sang to the tune as he danced with Gina:

"There was an old lady of Monterey,
Who lived in a shoe and sang all day,
She sang so well and she sang so long,
They never could tell why she sang this song."

Gina had to laugh as he swung her with her feet off the floor and kept singing.

"I had a pig with a long white tail,
Fat as a hog and fast as a snail,
Rode that pig at the county fair,
Won a prize as the cutest pair."

As the music stopped, he did not set her down, and grinned. "You got to marry me, Gina."

"Why?"

"Because I'm wild about you."

She just laughed. "You big silly."

Later down at the creek as the sun moved into the western sky over the Rockies, the rifle contest ended with a buffalo hunter taking first prize and young cowhands claiming lesser prizes.

For the fast-draw contest, the crowd fell back down along the creek. The wooden wall blocked direct views from the tent area, but Creighton had moved west across the top of the slope to get a better view without the wall being an obstruction. He found himself a stump to sit on, and crossed his fingers that Lassiter would lose.

Suellen came walking all the way over to where he sat. He

stood, tipping his hat, gesturing to the stump.

"No, please sit," she said. "I just want to watch."

Creighton would not sit in the presence of a lady, and stood aside. He knew she didn't like or trust him, but this was the only spot above the creek where one could easily see the fast draw. He wanted to say "I'm sorry," but it would have been meaningless to her.

They stood six feet apart, watching. Finally, a weary Suellen did sit on the stump.

Down at the creek, the judge, a chubby merchant, reminded the contestants they could only use single action revolvers and there were no second chances.

Lassiter came down from the upper crowd. Ben had his back to him when Higgins said quietly, "Here comes Lassiter."

Afraid a lifetime of fury would overcome him, Ben prepared not to meet Lassiter eye to eye. Not now. Not yet.

Standing back with Higgins, Tom watched Ben check his weapons.

I sure hope he really is my son, Tom silently prayed.

Five contestants were ahead of Lassiter and Ben.

All the while, Ben stood with his back to where Lassiter was preening.

Each of the first five shooters started with a whiskey bottle tossed high. The first three hit their target with their fast draw. The other two each missed and were ruled out. The next round followed with two empty ink bottles thrown upward. Only one hit both. But the final round was three empty perfume bottles, very small against the fading sun. The last shooter was also eliminated.

Now it was Ben and Lassiter. Ben avoided the man's gaze as he waved him on ahead. Lassiter snickered, telling himself his aim would be so perfect, the kid lawman would flub every shot.

Overconfident, Lassiter hit the whiskey bottle and then both ink bottles. When it came to the three tiny perfume flasks, Lassiter preened and strutted, as if to say, *watch this, you losers.*

The three flasks now sailed high in the air. They glistened in the sunlight. Lassiter drew fast and fired. He hit two but missed one. Against the rules, he fired again, but it hit the ground still intact. His horror and fury made him look ready to explode.

The crowd fell so silent, it was obvious they were now terrified. No one dared laugh. It would be up to the lawman now, but if he missed, it could get volatile until one came out ahead. Higgins hid his smile, as did Tom. Ben stayed somber.

Lassiter stood furious and alone for a long moment. He took time to reload his six-gun, apparently as a routine, but not in his ugly mind. He could not lose, not ever, no matter what he had to do from now on to save face.

From his view up the slope, Creighton smiled, happy to see Lassiter set back for a change. Suellen, her back to the rancher, smiled briefly, but now prayed Ben would finish as the winner. She soon realized her hands were turning white as they gripped her knees through her skirts.

Emma and Leslie, waiting in the tent, each with a lemonade, were silent and sober, unable to see what was happening. Creighton would happily bring back the news.

Down at the contest, the nervous judge cleared his throat. "It's now between Mr. Lassiter and the marshal."

Everyone backed further away. Lassiter, off by himself, looked as if he might draw on Ben at any moment. The gunman bit his lip as he yearned to see Ben miss more than one bottle.

Ben, trying his best not to let painful memories slow his draw, was clear of the crowd and alone by the creek as the bottles were tossed.

Ben's six-gun flew into his hand. He hit the whiskey bottle easy and then the two ink bottles right after. Next were the three tiny perfume flasks.

Lassiter reeled at how fast Ben was. His fury ate at him from inside.

When the perfume flasks glittered in the late rays of the sun, Ben drew so fast, no one saw his hand move. All three flasks burst apart with a jingle, glass sprinkling down to the creek.

Lassiter choked in dismay. Yes, he had reloaded, but Ben had another loaded revolver in his left holster. Lassiter had never known failure, until now. He swore to himself it would not stay that way. It was an accident, a fluke. He would have to make it right and have the upper hand once more.

The crowd burst into applause. Ever afraid of Lassiter, they fell slowly silent as they saw his power deflated by the amazing skill of the young marshal.

The nervous judge handed Ben a blue ribbon. "You can claim your saddle up at the judge's tent, son. Congratulations."

Ben shook the judge's hand, then turned to see the pride in Higgins' face and an even greater joy in Tom's expression. Ben reloaded his right revolver and holstered it. It might be expected that the winner would shake hands with the loser, but not this time.

Lassiter did not meet Ben's gaze as he turned and stomped up the rise. Already, he had a deadly plan. He was aware no one dared laugh, but he scowled, for Creighton had better not be smiling. This was only a temporary setback, a big surprise, and Lassiter would not let it stay that way.

Seeing Creighton standing near where Suellen sat, Lassiter turned toward the tents. Creighton, hat in hand, took a few steps to follow, then turned to her.

"Tell your friend, the marshal, I'm glad he won."

She nodded and stood as Creighton walked away. She couldn't quite figure him out. He had wielded deadly power since moving to Hang Town country, and could have caused her father's death. Yet he seemed to not be suffering from that particular guilt when he was near her. Only some kind of misery.

Suellen felt grateful that Ben had won, but now she knew his life was in danger. She would lose a lot of sleep from worry.

At the creek, with Lassiter out of the way, the crowd gathered around Ben with handshakes and slaps on the shoulder, then headed up the slope and back to the food.

Ben, Higgins, and Tom were left alone by the stream.

"Now you're in for it," Higgins said to Ben. "You shamed Lassiter, and he's gonna want to get even, but he won't play fair."

Ben, stunned by his win, could only murmur his thanks. He found the judge's box seat and sat on it. Tom, full of silent admiration, still did not have his burning questions answered.

When Lassiter reached the tent, Creighton was waiting and stood fighting his pleasure. As Lassiter grimly came over to them, Leslie looked down, and Emma looked odd.

"Bad luck," Creighton said, forcing a frown.

Lassiter nodded to him to come aside. Creighton walked

with Lassiter so the women could not hear over the music and crowd noise.

Lassiter sneered. "Let's see how he does tomorrow, man-to-man."

"You're calling him out?"

"Isn't that what you want?"

Creighton wavered. "I just want him to leave."

"He's not riding out of here with everyone thinking he's faster," Lassiter snarled. "And no man has ever taken me down in the street."

Lassiter, storming off, headed toward the tables and drinks.

Creighton stood quiet a moment, leery of his hired gun, and becoming sour. *I don't trust you, Lassiter. You only work for money. You have no loyalty. And that's why I'm going to stay armed, every minute. And I won't cry if you lose your big fight.*

Creighton wanted to be rid of Lassiter, but there had never been a chance until now. Warming to the kid lawman, he returned to the women in the big tent.

Down by the creek, Tom, Higgins, and Ben, seated on a wooden box, remained alone.

Ben could not believe he had actually out-shot his tormentor. It left him numb but eternally grateful that his prayers had been answered. It didn't erase the pain of his gasping for air when Lassiter pulled his head out of the trough. It didn't wash away all of the dreadful times. But winning the contest had brought some sweet kind of retribution that he now savored.

"Did you see Lassiter's face?" Higgins chuckled.

"Mighty fancy shooting," Tom said.

"Thanks" Ben replied, still in shock. "Maybe it was luck."

"I know better," Higgins said.

Ben shrugged, slowly getting to his feet.

"And there's some pretty fancy desserts going to waste up there," Higgins added.

Tom then hesitated. "Marshal, I have a serious problem and would like to talk with you in private."

Higgins adjusted his hat. "I'll try to leave some pie for you fellahs."

They waited until Higgins was out of earshot on his way up the grade.

Ben walked with Tom east along the creek, far away from the noisy crowd on the hill and with no one in Creighton's tent able to see them. The children were gone. The two men were alone as twilight fell.

Ben had no thoughts on what Tom's problem was, but he was glad for a stroll that kept him from being up where men would still slap him on the back. That would only enrage Lassiter more.

Still reeling from being near the gunman, Ben didn't care if any words were said now. He felt exhaustion down to his boots.

Tom, crumbling inside, fought for courage to face the next few minutes.

TEN

Ben, overwhelmed at beating Lassiter, something he had wanted all his adult life, felt on reflection that maybe this win would only stoke the fire. There was no telling what Lassiter might do to save face.

Walking east along the creek with Tom, Ben felt drained, but he liked this man.

"Marshal, I'll get right to the point."

Tom stopped, not looking directly at Ben, who paused near him.

Tom suddenly turned further away, his right shoulder toward Ben, and staring into the distant woods. The words came hard because he knew he could be wrong about Ben being his son. He could only hope and pray.

"I'm Tom Landry."

Ben, awestruck, couldn't grasp the sudden news. *My God, my father! He's here? This big Texan is my real dad?*

Ben fought the urge to throw his arms around the man. Someone above could be watching.

Ben found his voice. "You're my father?"

"I only found out this morning. But how did you know?"

"Higgins, he had a friend who told him."

They shook hands so firmly, it hurt. Knowing someone could be watching from up the slope, they separated. Ben yearned to sit down, but there was no spot from which he could get back up, given how overwhelmed he felt.

"Does my mother know?" Ben asked.

"About me being here, yes. About you being alive, no."

"She's not well, hasn't been for years."

"I could see that. So, why did you run away from home? Lassiter told her you had stolen some money and took off."

"My God, no," Ben said as his story burst into words. "I was a skinny little kid. Lassiter liked to shove my head in the water trough when I talked back. He beat me where it wouldn't show. Each time my mother lost another kid, he told me it was my fault, and how she didn't want me anymore, the same thing he always said. One night he said to get and never come back or he would kill me. So, I left when I was twelve and changed my name."

Tom, startled and hurting for that little boy, waited for Ben to continue.

Ben shook his head. "I didn't know why he hated me until I learned about you. It was because I was your son. And not his."

He told of how Lassiter forced Leslie to continue trying to have children, and how she became more sickly as time passed. Ben told more of why and how he left, what happened at the river, and how everyone thought he was dead.

The more Tom heard, the more furious he became, but he remained silent as Ben continued his life story.

Ben spoke of the cowman with the trail herd who took him in hand. "Then a few years later, I turned lawman."

"And Mr. Higgins?"

Ben nodded. "Only friend I ever had. When everyone thought I had drowned, one of Lassiter's men told him about you. Man named Boggs."

Tom reacted with surprise. "Boggs, he's the reason I'm free."

"But how?"

"Seems he was one of the men who lied on the witness stand. But when he was dying, he confessed in writing to the sheriff up here in Hang Town. And that sheriff sent the news to Texas. A Sheriff Long."

"My God," Ben muttered, thinking of Suellen.

"Thanks to him, I was given a pardon, but until I find out who did the killing, my name will never be clear."

Ben continued his own story, how when Higgins had learned about Ben's real father, he thought it was too late because Ben had supposedly drowned. Further, Ben related how Higgins, seeing the name of a deputy named Ben Cross in the paper, thought it a coincidence. But when Higgins had learned of Tom's pardon, he had tracked Ben down, just to make sure.

"No one expected you so soon," Ben said.

"I was actually pardoned a month ago. The newspaper release was late as part of the plan. As set by the governor and the prison superintendent."

"They went out of their way to help you?"

"Because I was a Texan." Tom tugged at his hat brim and cleared his throat. "Your mother and I were teenagers when we eloped. Her uncle caught us. He claimed I had shot and robbed his brother. They were going to hang me on the spot."

"But?"

"I figure she had to agree to the annulment just to save my life, but I was still railroaded. That was bad enough, but forcing her to marry a man like Lassiter when her uncle could have found someone decent?"

"Who do you think did the killing?"

"I aim to find out," Tom said, grateful that his son assumed his innocence.

"But you're not safe here."

"What about you? Out-shooting Lassiter won't make him love you very much."

Ben nodded with a sheepish grin. "He's also had his eye on that silver saddle. Now he's going to find another way to get it."

Tom looked up, toward the back of the main tent. "She's still beautiful."

Ben worried. "It's not safe for her to know who I am. I don't want Lassiter to know until I'm ready. And you'll be safer if you don't say who you are, not to anyone else."

"You may be right."

Ben stood looking at Tom, saw similarities. "No wonder I got so big."

Tom sniffed. "I'm right proud of you, son."

"When this is over, the saddle is yours."

At that moment, they saw Higgins coming down the slope to be sure Ben was okay.

"We can trust him," Ben assured his father.

They stood waiting as Higgins came to a halt in front of them. Knowing something was up, the older man looked from one to other with anticipation.

"Mr. Higgins, this here's my father, Tom Landry."

"Holy cow," Higgins said, shaking Tom's hand. "Now I got to look after the both of you."

At the end of the day, with dwindling food, the end of the games, and the last of the firecrackers, a weary crowd finished off the deserts as night fell. The Creightons and Lassiters vanished in the departing crowd.

Ben, Tom, and Higgins walked over to join Gina and Matlock near the judge's tent. The gray haired merchant left the door wide open for Ben to retrieve the glittering silver saddle. Suellen walked over to join them.

Higgins gestured. "Ben won the saddle."

Suellen had to take a moment to admire a man who could beat Lassiter.

Higgins added, "Lassiter was outright humiliated."

"Marshal," Matlock said, hugging a bashful Gina to his side, "would you please tell this little lady to marry me?"

Ben had to smile and nod, but Suellen spoke up.

"You'll have to go all the way to Butte City for a preacher."

Gina could not move from the circle of Matlock's arm. "I haven't said yes."

Matlock laughed. "Little lady, you know you're crazy about me."

As he bounced her up and down, Gina giggled. "Okay, so I can't help myself."

"Yippee!" Matlock said, whirling her around.

It was a joyful thing to watch, but Tom suffered in silence. He wanted very much to thank Suellen for her father's courageous act to free him, whether or not it had caused the lawman's death. He wanted her to know of his gratitude, but the timing could be wrong, and so he only smiled at her.

Ben and Higgins knew what was on Tom's mind, but they said nothing.

Just then, the surly Zeke Hogan walked over to them.

"Marshal," he snickered, "Lassiter will meet you at high noon tomorrow, in front of the hotel. He's going to show you how guns are more than play things. The whole town will be watching you go down. Unless you up and run away."

Zeke sauntered off as Suellen fretted. "If you win tomorrow, the Hogans will be hiding nearby to cut you down."

Higgins frowned, shook his head. "We'll make it fair."

"Count me in," Matlock said, releasing Gina but holding her hand.

"I have my rifle," Tom said. "I'll cover the roofs around the hotel."

"At least the sun will be overhead," Higgins said.

Suellen fretted, aghast. "Marshal, you're out of your mind! Lassiter has never lost a gunfight."

No, Ben told himself, *but this is where I've been heading since I was twelve.*

Higgins tried to stay calm. "Ben's a second faster."

Matlock tipped his finger under Gina's chin. "I got to do this, little lady. You go on home. We got to go look over the streets. And alleys."

Gina, although admiring the men for their bravery, had the same dread as Suellen. Neither one wanted anyone to die, except maybe Lassiter.

"So, we have a plan," Higgins said as they all nodded.

Staring at Ben who had already touched her heart, Suellen

could not control herself. She walked right up to him, pulled his head down and kissed him on the cheek. "I'll be watching that sleazy Porter."

His face reddening, Ben felt his throat go so dry, it hurt.

Gina dragged Suellen away.

Higgins grinned at Ben. "She still thinks you're pretty."

Ben knew his face was flushed in many colors. With only those cleaning the tables in view, he recovered and stood alone with Higgins, Tom, and Matlock.

"She's right about Porter," Higgins said. "And we'll be covering your back."

Tom could hardly contain himself. He had so much pride in this young man and his friends. Yet, now he feared losing the son he never knew he had. He lingered back with Ben as Higgins, understanding, led Matlock away.

Tom turned to Ben, who felt his father's pride and fear. Neither could speak. They clasped hands in a firm grip. Understanding passed between them.

Slowly, they turned to follow the others.

Out at the Creighton Ranch that night, Lassiter and Creighton were alone on the porch by the soft glow of the lamp. Lassiter still burned from his loss in the contest. Creighton secretly loved that Lassiter had lost face.

"Can you take him?" Creighton asked at length.

"Easy, but I got backup."

"If you have help, folks will say you were scared."

"But I'd be dead, so why would I care?"

"So, you may lose?"

"I said I can take him."

You're scared, Creighton mused to himself. *That kid has made you turn yellow.*

Lassiter folded his arms and stared at the distant corrals as his own mind considered what he could do if the unthinkable happened. Lassiter had never been this nervous about a fight, but if he lost, he was not going down easy. He vowed to get even with Creighton with his dying breath. Creighton would pay for all his wrongs, including stealing his wife's ranch.

Neither man knew that Ben was Leslie's son, nor did they know that Tom Landry was here a month early.

They only knew that the fastest gun in the west would be facing a kid lawman, a kid who won the fast-draw contest and now had Lassiter's saddle.

Creighton hid his delight. Lassiter hid his growing aggravation.

Inside the house, Leslie excused herself from the cranky Emma and went to her room. Emma had her own fussing to do.

No one on the ranch knew Tom had arrived, but she did, and her heart was sick with dread and fear that he would be discovered and killed.

I still love him, she thought, amazed at how twenty-five years had faded away at the sound of his voice, however deep it had become. *Dear God, I love him even now, because I've never loved anyone else. Ever.*

She had no way of knowing the young marshal, whom she had not seen because of the crowd and her seclusion in the tent, was, in fact, her long-lost son. She only knew there would be a killing in the streets of Hang Town.

Either she would be a widow, or the young lawman would be dead in the streets.

If her husband survived, Tom would not have a chance if discovered.

She knelt by the bed and whispered her prayers. She could not ask that the kid lawman win the fight. She could not ask that her husband would die. She could only pray for Tom's safety and for her own strength to handle whatever happened at noon on Tuesday.

She hurried to be asleep before Lassiter came to their room.

When he later entered as the lamp burned low, Lassiter removed his gun belt and sat in his big chair. He studied this beautiful woman as she slept. She was his, now and forever. No one else would ever have her.

As he pulled off his boots, Lassiter thought again of his failure at the contest and felt it had only been a fluke. Not a religious man, he lived only for his own needs and wants. He could count on no one but himself.

Lassiter sat staring at his hands, slowly regaining his confidence.

No one had ever beaten him, man-to-man. And they never would.

ELEVEN

As high noon approached on Tuesday, the streets of Hang Town were lined with mostly men, while women and children stayed in doorways and at windows. Except in front of the hotel where a roof overhang, designed to protect arriving guests from the weather, shaded spectators, including the Creightons, from the sun.

Jed Creighton, Emma at his side in her glamour and with a parasol, stood in the front of the crowd. To Jed's right, Deputy Porter waited, well-armed. To their left and in front, Leslie sat in a chair with a blanket over her. Next to Leslie, Suellen, gun belt under her jacket, scanned areas that could be hiding spots, and also kept an eye on Porter, some twenty feet away beyond the Creightons. At her side, Gina also watched for any danger.

To the east and away from the crowd, back in a doorway, Tom held his rifle and studied the rooftops. Unseen in other alleyways, Higgins and Matlock hunted the Hogans and any others bent on ambush.

Matlock was first to come upon a Hogan. From the rear of

the alley opposite the hotel and east of it, Bart Hogan hovered at the edge of the street entrance with his six-gun, which he dropped when Matlock's pistol jammed into his neck.

Opposite the hotel but to the west of the crowd, Higgins slipped up behind Bo and jammed his revolver into the man's back. "Drop it." Startled, Bo let his weapon fall to the ground. Higgins marched him around behind the building, unseen by the crowd, to join Matlock.

In the street, coming west from the direction of the sheriff's office, Lassiter was putting on a show. He stopped to preen, spotting Porter in front of the hotel. Besides the Hogans, the gunman was counting on the deputy to be his backup.

Lassiter had regained his bravado. He knew he could make men turn tail just by intimidating them.

This is it, Lassiter told himself. *Don't give the kid a chance.*

Coming up the street from the bridge, heading east toward the hotel, Ben walked slowly. He relived his life over and over: the times his face was shoved into the water trough so long, he thought he would die; the beatings that left no marks; the continued isolation of a young boy from his own mother; the insults and lies that led to his running away.

Leslie, seated in the shade of the hotel overhang, looked into the street where her husband Lassiter slowly moved toward his opponent, the young marshal. She saw the lawman's size, then his face shaded by his hat. His face! Something in this husky young man still held the image of her little boy. Now he shoved his hat back as he walked.

Her heart near burst. "My God. It's my son!"

Leslie half-rose but couldn't get to her feet. She tried to spot Tom, but her view was blocked by the Creightons to her right. Unaware that Tom already knew their son was alive, she became frantic, feeling helpless. *Dear God, protect our boy.*

Ben, still eighty feet from Lassiter, kept walking slowly.

Tom, off by himself in the alley entrance next to the hotel, looked up, saw Zeke Hogan on the opposite roof prone with his rifle aimed at Ben. Before Zeke could fire, Tom raised his rifle and shot him. The crowd jumped, startled.

Zeke rose crazily from the roof, dropped his rifle and spun off the building, crashing down onto the boardwalk. He landed with a thud, then rolled aside.

Lassiter stopped, thinking he still had two aces in the hole, but then he heard Bo's outcry, turned half around to see Bo and Bart in custody with their hands tied behind them, standing further back and to his right with Matlock and Higgins in charge.

Now Lassiter had only two allies: the deputy over by Creighton, and perhaps Creighton himself. No one noticed Suellen moving behind the crowd and up behind Porter.

The deputy put his hand on his holster, until Suellen stuck her pistol in his back.

"Don't even think about it," she murmured, just loud enough for him to hear.

A coward by nature, Porter dropped his hand, but her pistol remained pressed against his spine.

Lassiter saw that Porter had been stopped. He saw no help in Creighton's gaze.

For the first time in his deadly career, Lassiter broke into a sweat. He had seen Ben's skill with the fast draw and his flawless aim. His backup was no more. This was it, but he called on himself to once again prove he was the very best.

He recalled the faces of the men he had shot down over the years. He regained his confidence as the confrontation became imminent.

As he realized Creighton might be enjoying this, Lassiter vowed that he would not die now or in some distant future, not without taking his revenge on the man who had stolen Leslie's ranch. At the same time, he told himself he was going to win, just as he always had.

I'm going to kill me a marshal, Lassiter silently vowed.

When Ben was within forty feet of his tormentor, Ben fought for the right words. Words to let Lassiter know his brutality, lies, and plans to be rid of a little skinny kid had failed.

"Not so easy now," he said aloud to Lassiter. "When I was twelve, you half-drowned me in the trough, time and again. You lied and tormented me until I ran away."

Lassiter stopped dead in his tracks. *No, it couldn't be.*

Leslie called out, "Please, Harry, he's my son!"

"He's lying," Lassiter shouted to her. "The kid is dead!"

She half-rose from her chair. "No!"

Lassiter hesitated, still not believing this big man was the same little boy.

"She's right," Tom said, stepping forward with his rifle near Suellen and the deputy, then moving to the edge of the boardwalk where Leslie could see him. "I'm his father. Tom Landry."

Lassiter stopped, twisted to stare at Tom, even as Jed Creighton gasped.

Staring at the big bearded man with the rifle, Creighton could barely handle the moment. He had hated Landry all these years for killing Amos. Not a killer by nature, the rancher yet felt the rage rising within him, the same rage when he had found his kid brother in the barn. He put his hand on his holster but waited on Lassiter, who still faced the kid marshal.

Leslie stared across at Tom, the man she had loved as a teen. He looked so big and handsome, so strong, and yet in his face, she saw he was the same, and she knew then that she still loved him as if no years had passed.

Tom kept his gaze on the street, rifle leveled at his hip. He dared not lose his concentration by letting Leslie distract him.

Lassiter had a flash vision of the skinny kid he had despised for being another man's son. It fired him up so that he regained his power and readied for the kill. He forgot the contest and Ben's skill. He forgot everything except that he had never lost a duel and would not lose now, because this kid had to die once and for all.

All chips were down, and Lassiter drew faster than ever.

Ben's Colt leaped in his hand and fired before Lassiter could pull the trigger.

Stunned, all watching stood speechless.

Hit hard in the chest, a shocked Lassiter dropped to his knees, letting his weapon fall aside. His eyes were wild.

Ben walked right over to him, Colt pointed at him. "Who hanged the sheriff? And why?"

Already dying, Lassiter sputtered. "The Hogans. On account of him getting Landry out..."

Up on the boardwalk, Tom heard the truth, and Suellen wilted.

Ben persisted with the mortally-wounded Lassiter.

"Who shot and robbed Amos Creighton?"

Dazed with blurring vision, Lassiter knew he was dying, but revenge on Creighton drove his voice to be loud and clear.

"We didn't know Amos was back from town. He turned up the lamp. Saw us rolling in the hay, and he laughed. When he walked away, Emma grabbed my pistol off the post and shot him in the back."

Silence fell heavy in the street, even as Creighton paled in shock.

Lassiter suddenly repeated as loud as he could. "Emma shot him."

"Liar!" Creighton said, pulling his revolver, hammer back.

Emma grabbed her husband's arm. "No, Jed, I love him!"

She struggled over the weapon, turning it away from Lassiter and upward, causing Creighton to lose his balance. The Colt came down, went off, blasting Emma in the chest.

Startled, Emma, crazy-eyed, started to fall.

Creighton caught her as he gained his footing. The woman he loved, the one he had committed crime after crime to please, this woman who had betrayed him from the start, was dying in his arms. He lowered her to the boardwalk.

As Emma passed, she still whispered, "I love him."

Creighton, numb with shock, knelt on one knee at her side. For all these years, he had believed Tom Landry guilty. How he could ever make it up to the man, he didn't know. All that mattered at the moment was that the woman he had loved was leaving him forever. Regrets would haunt him, but God help him, he loved her even now.

In the street, Lassiter, still on his knees, looked toward the fallen Emma with no regret, as she had been a one-time roll in the hay. He had loved only Leslie, as strongly as he had hated that she had borne another man's son. A runt of a kid he had driven away because he was sick at the sight of him.

Lassiter's vision blurred as he stared up at Ben, fighting the image of a little boy dancing in the face of the tall lawman.

Lassiter slowly leaned forward, falling lifeless and facedown in the dusty street.

Ben slowly holstered his weapon with a heavy heart.

The spectators, the show now over, gradually left the scene.

On the boardwalk, the doctor came out to kneel and check on Emma, then stood once more. "I'm sorry, Mr. Creighton."

Two men beckoned by the doctor came to carry Emma's body inside the hotel. The rancher slowly followed, shoulders hunched over. Before returning to the hotel, the doctor walked out to check on Lassiter, then shook his head and turned back.

In the street, Ben felt no joy, only relief from his miserable memories. It had been some solace to let Lassiter know his punishment for a little boy had failed. Now he only felt glad to have his father hurry to his side. They both looked from the fallen killer to the tearful Leslie, half-rising from her chair on the boardwalk.

Tom put his hand on Ben's shoulder with relief and pride.

Then Tom turned back to the boardwalk where Leslie sat. As he neared her, he was stunned by the closeup of her lovely face, his heart racing. He knelt on one knee at the side of her chair as she sat back. Her hesitant smile, a mixture of being suddenly widowed and at the same time trembling with joy, left her breathless.

Tom took her hand and kissed it. Tears trickled down her face. They both looked toward where their son stood as other men came to view the dead man.

Ben waited in the street until Lassiter was carried away, along with Zeke.

Feeling drained, Ben turned to see Higgins and Matlock with the prisoners. Ben tensed as he looked over at Porter, but he soon realized he did not have to worry about the deputy. He almost grinned at the sight.

Suellen stood behind Porter, prodding him with her pistol. "You have prisoners, Deputy, and I suggest you do your duty before that federal marshal locks you up instead."

Porter, who always knew which way the wind blew, already figured Creighton would no longer offer compensation. Steeling himself, he crossed over to help Matlock march the prisoners to jail. Suellen stood back as she holstered her weapon.

Ben finally walked over to where Tom knelt by Leslie.

Ben bent over to hug her and kiss her forehead. "Mom, you can call me Ben. After Grandpa."

Leslie sobbed. Tom, his eyes wet, stood up as Ben stayed on one knee.

"I'll be back," Tom said, worried about Creighton. He headed into the hotel lobby where Emma lay on a couch, covered by a blanket. The rancher sat in a chair, head down, but he straightened to look up at Tom.

With great regret and heartache, the rancher knew what he had to say.

"Landry, I was wrong," Creighton said, tears trickling down his face. "Lassiter saw Emma murder my kid brother and took the money pouch so it would look like a robbery, and then he beat it back to town knowing I would send for him. And when you became an easy target, he pretended to search your gear so he could hide it in your saddlebags."

Tom didn't answer, somehow feeling more sorry for the rancher than himself.

Creighton looked so beaten, Tom had no heart left to berate him, but walked closer to put his hand on the beaten man's shoulder.

Tom then walked back outside to be with his son and Leslie.

Higgins crossed over to join Suellen as they watched the tearful reunion.

"A long time coming," he said to her.

Suellen nodded. "Amen."

"I hope your father knows he let a good man out of prison."

"I'm sure he does," she said, brushing away a tear.

Gina came to their side from the rear of the crowd but suddenly brightened. She saw Matlock coming back out of the sheriff's office down the street. She hurried over and all the way into his arms. Matlock hugged her, then showed her the sheriff's watch.

Back in front of the hotel, Suellen felt drained even as Matlock, Gina at his side, came over to give her the gold timepiece. She took it with added misery and put it in her pocket.

Ben and Tom hovered around Leslie, now a family.

"Feel sorry for my Uncle Jed," Leslie said. "Everything he did, it was all for Emma."

The elderly doctor came out of the hotel and over to Leslie. "I'm afraid your uncle's likely to harm himself."

Leslie started to rise, but Tom stopped her. "I'll go."

Tom left Leslie with Ben and followed the doctor back inside the lobby. No one was in view except Creighton seated near the sofa where Emma lay, still covered with blankets. Next to him, the elderly doctor stood, nagging.

"We have to take her away."

Creighton bitterly shook his head.

Tom signaled the doctor to leave and pulled up a chair just behind the rancher's right side.

Creighton, unaware Tom had replaced the doctor, and unmindful of his own tears, muttered, "I was a fool."

"No, sir," Tom said.

Startled, Creighton wiped at his eyes, twisted about and stared at Tom, then choked on his words. "I can never make it up to you."

"Yes, you can."

Creighton hesitated, even now in his grief. Ever used to everyone wanting something from him, he braced himself for some kind of demand for money. He would not be inclined to resist because this man, Tom Landry, had suffered at his hands and had spent twenty-five years in prison for something Emma had done.

Tom, hat in hand, leaned forward from his chair. He felt pain for the rancher, despite his own hurt and loss.

"I need a job," Tom said.

"A job?" Creighton stammered.

"I want to ask Leslie to marry me, but I have nothing to offer."

For a long time, Creighton could only stare at the man he had wronged.

"A job?" Creighton repeated. "That's all you want?"

"Yes, sir."

Overcome with admiration, Creighton calmed himself. "You know cattle?"

"No, sir, but I'm good with horses."

"Horses," Creighton said, fumbling for words. "We have a lot of saddle horses. Some colts."

"I mean racing blood."

The rancher perked up. "Yes, I've thought about it, and I know of a good stud. We can bring him up from Cheyenne. Round up some fine brood mares."

"Sure would appreciate it."

Creighton drew a deep breath. "You're restoring my faith in people."

Tom held out his hand, which Creighton took in a weak handshake.

"And in yourself," Tom said. "Because Leslie will need you."

Humbled by Tom's words, Creighton hardly reacted as the doctor came in with two men assisting him.

"Let me take over," the doctor insisted once again.

Creighton stood, this time resigned to it, but shaking all over as he saw them carry his wife's body away. Tom took his arm. Crumbling inside, Creighton had entered the lobby with no desire to live, but now he reminded himself he had always been a fighter, so maybe he could face what lay ahead.

As Tom led him across the lobby toward the entrance, Creighton mumbled, "You're a better man than I ever was."

"So, I got the job?" Tom asked with a smile.

Creighton fumbled with his answer. "Yeah, sure."

They paused as a worried Leslie came into the lobby and joined them.

Tom held Creighton's left arm, Leslie his right.

Creighton, though suffering from shame and loss, looked at her face where the light of a new beginning was shining in her eyes.

"Leslie, I did wrong by you, down in Texas."

"That was Texas," she said brightly. "This is Montana. Big sky country."

"I have a job," Tom said to her. "Your uncle and I, we're going to raise race horses. Heck, maybe we'll even have one fit for the Kentucky Derby."

Uncle Jed nodded as Leslie put her arm around him.

Late that afternoon under a cloudy sky, Lassiter and Zeke Hogan were buried without ceremony. A short while after, Creighton witnessed the burial of his wife while standing alone. Leslie, Tom, and Ben were among the witnesses waiting some ten feet away, including only a few men from town.

Creighton had bitter thoughts as he stared down at her marker. *Beloved wife? Yes, but I went against my brother Ben and married you, because I loved you. Every rotten thing I ever did was for you. Stealing the ranch from Leslie was the worst of all. But you wanted it. You wanted everything, and I had to keep finding ways to pay for it, and some of what I did, I'll always regret. But now I know it was Lassiter all along. You played me for a fool. Allowed me to send an innocent young man to prison for something you had done. But, God help me, I still love you.*

Creighton worried Leslie, still afraid he would end his own life, a concern she had voiced to Tom. The two of them came to his side and escorted him back to the street. Ben stayed out of the circle, watching his father and mother with pride, but from a distance.

As the small crowd drifted away, Leslie put her arm around her uncle.

"We're having an early supper in the cantina. Can you join us?" Tom asked.

Creighton hesitated, could not believe the kindness and turn of events. "I'd be honored."

That evening at the entrance to the noisy cantina with a sprinkle of rain beginning, Leslie, Ben, Gina, and Matlock entered ahead of the others. Lingering outside in the shadows, Suellen was stopped by Creighton and Tom.

Tom removed his hat. "Your father is the reason I'm here. He sent a letter with Boggs' confession, all the way to Huntsville. He was a brave man."

Suellen, deeply touched, reached out to Tom and squeezed his hand briefly.

Creighton, emotional, wiped away a tear. "I can only say I'm sorry. I was getting old and tired, and I let Lassiter have a free hand."

They knew that he really meant Emma had driven him to the point of no return.

Suellen, eyes wet, shook her head. "Let's all start over."

Falling rain drove them inside the noisy cantina. The crowd didn't seem to remember the gunfight. Laughter, arm wrestling, flirtations, clumsy dancers, all reflected a new beginning. Guitars played lively music.

At a separate, long table with some privacy, supper was pleasant with Leslie seated next to her uncle and close to Tom, holding his hand under the table. Creighton, at the head of the table with Leslie and Tom to his left, could barely handle his food. Higgins was at Creighton's right, and next to him, Suellen, then Ben, and at the end of the table, Gina and Matlock acting like teenagers.

The widowed proprietor, Mrs. Perez, dark eyes flashing and looking particularly fetching, fussed over the diners. She aimed her attention at Higgins but now included the rancher, who had no clue as to her interest.

Gina beamed. "Mr. Higgins, I'm marrying this big lunkhead," she said of the grinning Matlock at her side, "so, would you give me away?"

Higgins accepted with a big grin.

Realizing Leslie looked healthier by the minute, Creighton silently prayed for forgiveness and with thanks for this turn of events.

Suddenly, Tom rose, pulled back his chair, and then knelt down in front of Leslie. "I can't wait."

Leslie gazed down at him with a great love in her heart, wondering.

"I know you're just now a widow, but I don't figure you were ever married to anyone else."

She silently agreed, but this was so unexpected, she could only stare at him.

"Marry me. Again."

Leslie could not find her voice, and he feared rejection.

"Leslie, I never stopped loving you."

She flushed. "Oh, Tom, I'd marry you a hundred times over."

Now he rose high enough to kiss her, causing both to shiver with joy. In that emotional touching of their lips, twenty-five years melted away. It was yesterday to both of them.

Watching, Ben fought the wet in his eyes. He saw Creighton wipe away his tears.

That's when Leslie turned to smile at her uncle. "Uncle Jed, would you give me away?"

Creighton, speechless, could only nod as Tom returned to his chair but kept holding her hand. Leslie's health seemed bound to improve with the glow in her cheeks and sparkle in her green eyes.

Matlock and Gina chipped in. "Can we make it a double wedding?" Matlock asked.

"I want Leslie to get well first," Tom said.

Gina giggled. "I can wait."

Reluctant, but under her spell, Matlock had to nod.

After much joy, Tom turned to look at his son across the table. "What about you, Ben? How long can you be here with us?"

"The boss sent word," Ben said. "He says I can stay here and open an office in town."

Tom and Leslie looked more than happy at the news.

"And go after vigilantes?" Higgins asked of Ben, who nodded.

"I can help with that," Creighton said.

Ben raised his shoulders with pride as he zeroed in on Tom. "And I told the boss my name was now Ben Cross Landry. If that's okay with you, Dad?"

Tom flushed with pride. "Thank you, son."

Leslie could not stop her tears.

Nor could Creighton.

TWELVE

As the summer turned into fall at the Creighton Ranch, Leslie and Tom waited for Leslie's health to improve, which it did, stunning the doctor, although they all knew in their hearts that her illness had been caused by Lassiter with his overbearing demands.

Meanwhile, Tom worked with Creighton on the ranch, learning about cattle as they went along, impressing the rancher, who also admired Tom's skill with horses. A stud was on its way up from Cheyenne. Brood mares were coming from Denver.

Leslie, Suellen, and Gina organized a drastic change to the Creighton Ranch House. Women from town and the surrounding ranches came to help. Some accepted pieces of rosewood furniture. The piano would be donated to a new church under construction in town where a new minister would be called. Many of the other items would soon be for sale in town.

No one wanted Emma's gowns because they had all disliked her. Everyone also knew Emma had looked down her nose at Indian women and anyone else who didn't meet her standards, such as Gina, and the Chinese ladies. Which is why a ranch woman had the answer for all the Paris finery. "Give them to the army, and they'll send them to the reservation where they can be cut up and put to better use as needed clothing."

Leslie was delighted and happy to agree.

The servants were reduced to a housekeeper and the cook. The two maids found work in town at the hotel.

* * * * *

That September in 1881, under an overcast sky in late afternoon, a double wedding with over three hundred guests took place on the Creighton Ranch. In front of the garden, flowers decorated an arbor and sheltering tarps. Next to a wooden dance floor, tables of food had all the trimmings.

The ceremony was performed by the new minister.

Gina—lovely and bright in a colorful red and ivory gown—and Matlock were married first. He was stiff and barely fit into the largest suit available, and could hardly wait to tear off the coat. Higgins walked Gina down the flower-lined aisle.

Suellen—wearing powder blue to match her eyes—and a ranch lady were in waiting for both brides. Ben stood up for his father and for Matlock.

Leslie, healthy and gorgeous, wore an ivory wedding dress with lots of lace and whirling skirts. Her long veil dangled from a shiny tiara, dotted with emeralds the color of her brilliant eyes. Her uncle, his soul recovered, smiled as he escorted her to the altar.

Tom, looking particularly handsome in his dark suit, had such joy bursting within him, he could barely say his vows. Then he lifted Leslie in his arms and swing her about, and somehow, in those few moments, he was an eighteen-year-old apprentice smithy and she was a seventeen-year-old princess. They had their first dance in memory of the one they had as teens.

Jed Creighton, now sitting on the porch, smiled as he watched Leslie and Tom embrace. The crowd—mainly ranch hands and a few families from other ranches and town—ate heartily, danced to the fiddles, and made it a delightful time for all.

Mrs. Perez—pretty in dark green, her attention split between the cagey Higgins and the clueless rancher—had competition for the rancher from the doctor's widowed sister with flaming red hair.

As the fiddles started playing slow music, Tom led Leslie to the dance floor once again. Everyone could see they were so in love, and it was envied.

Leslie whispered. "I loved you on first sight, even when you stepped on my toes."

"You were the prettiest girl there," Tom said in a low voice. "You had me right off."

As they danced, Tom and Leslie also enjoyed seeing Matlock whirl Gina about.

Meanwhile in the chilling twilight, Suellen impatiently took Ben's arm and pulled him away from the crowd. He quickly sought to protect himself from her charms, which he had managed all afternoon by hanging with the other men.

"I have to talk to you," she said to Ben.

"I can't dance."

"I don't care."

Uneasy, Ben let her lead him out of earshot and into the far end of the garden. In the coming night with the last rays of the setting sun reaching through the clouds, she was gorgeous in a sparkling gold gown that matched the glitter of her long flowing hair.

Ben fought for resistance and tried not to meet her gaze.

"Listen to me," she said firmly. "I once told your mother if I ever met a man who would stand up to Lassiter, I'd marry him."

"Wait..."

"Wait for what?"

"I don't know, because..."

"At least six children from now, we'll be old, but not lonely."

Flustered, Ben could not find words. "But I..."

"Yes, I will marry you."

Ben had no answer, no fight left. They were spotted as he looked toward the distant dance floor where his mother, laughing, swayed in the arms of his grinning father. He saw Higgins' delight. Even Creighton looked touched. Matlock and Gina hugged and smiled as they shared in the joy. They had all been watching and hoping. They could not hear, but it was all so obvious.

Stunned where he stood, Ben could not move.

Suellen stood on her tiptoes. "I'm a dead shot, so you'd better kiss me."

Ben stammered. "But..."

Suellen pushed his hat back, pulled his head down, and kissed him on the lips.

Ben folded, gathered her up against him, his heart loud in his ears. As he kissed her, he realized that from the day he had seen her riding all golden into that red canyon, he had yearned for this moment.

The happy evening continued well into the night under a moonlit sky with lamps burning and a bonfire. Exhausted guests found benches where they could rest and chat.

Tom and Leslie walked over to where Creighton sat alone on the porch in the lamplight. He beamed at them with pride. *A long time coming*, he thought, finally able to forgive himself, hoping he had come up with a way to remedy the wrong.

"Tom, I've admired how you've taken to the ranch," Creighton said. "And you are better at training horses than any man I've known."

"Thank you, sir."

"I have something for you," the rancher said. He reached inside his jacket and took out a folded paper. " My lawyer said I now have a life estate that lets me live out my days on the ranch."

Leslie turned emotional. "You don't need that…"

"And," the rancher added, "the ranch now belongs to you and Tom."

Tom wilted with amazement and gratitude.

A startled Leslie moved forth to bend down and hug her uncle.

"I owe it to the both of you for the wrong I did," the rancher added. "And for saving my life, because I was ready to end it. Instead, now I have family."

"We'll make your family grow," Leslie promised.

Tom accepted the paper with great humility and shook his hand. "Thank you, sir. We will do our best to make you proud."

"Just let me spoil your kids," Creighton said as Leslie kissed him on the cheek. Then suddenly Creighton muttered, "Oh, no," looking past her.

They turned to see Mrs. Perez headed their way.

* * * * *

TWO YEARS LATER on the ranch, Leslie, still happily wed to Tom, was blooming with joy, having given birth to handsome twin boys one year back, and healthily pregnant again.

Resigned to his past mistakes, Jed Creighton would never forget his lost love, nor how she had betrayed him, but he was learning to be a better man, the man he would have been but for her. He had also gained weight from Mrs. Perez's weekly visits with her rich desserts, but that had abruptly ended when she married the town baker. However, the casseroles continued from the doctor's redhaired sister, who was slowly getting his attention.

Tom proudly handled the new colts, which would be widely sought by ranchers, and had welcomed visits from Goree, who felt nothing but pride. Tom and Creighton spent many days riding the trails together, enjoying the splendor.

Creighton often expressed his admiration to Tom. "I never met a horse whisperer before, but you're as close as they come."

Tom would shrug and redden but enjoyed Creighton's friendship. It had been a long time coming, but they had found a common ground, horses.

Living on the ranch in his own shack and retired from the railroad, Higgins was content and well-stocked with newspapers, quietly enjoying checkers with some of the cowhands, but eventually the new town leaders prevailed on him and Tom to oversee the reopening of the town's long shuttered newspaper. Tom had a hand in it, but only at the start.

Higgins was then promised a steady supply of ready print for his own nighttime reading, and once the new editor and printer were thriving, he retired back to his shack to enjoy an endless supply of papers and magazines. Except that the former Mrs. Perez, widowed again, was soon bringing him rich desserts.

U.S. Deputy Marshal Ben Cross Landry—assigned the territory with an office in town and still surprised by his wife Suellen—was the proud father of a young son with another on the way. Creighton spent hours with the boy at the small ranch Suellen had inherited, but also was in great demand on the home ranch as Leslie, pregnant again, needed help with their little boys.

Matlock, still wild about his bride Gina, was the father of twins, a boy and a girl. He was also town marshal and proud of it. He was so well liked, a house had been provided for them.

Porter had been asked to leave long ago, and the new county sheriff not only had two deputies, he had worked with Deputy U.S. Marshal Ben Cross Landry to rid the plains of vigilantes. Meanwhile, the Hogans were spending life in prison at Deer Lodge.

A new schoolmarm had cowboys courting her, and with the Fourth of July ahead of them once again, she was leading the decorating committee. The streets were peaceful, and Deacon Jones had returned to assist the new minister with the church.

The railroad had now crossed Montana and brought business and prosperity to the area. Simmons Flat was back in business with a fast-growing population. Hang Town was only a fading memory.

Montana would be a state in 1889, represented by Jed Creighton, then sixty-eight, who would finally give in and marry the doctor's very patient sister, so that she could accompany him to Washington, D. C.

* * * * *

As years passed, Ben and Suellen had added many rooms to the old house on the ranch she inherited. He would often sit by the fire in the evening, watching his lovely wife play a game with their six children—all boys, ages ten, eight, six, four, and a set of two-year-old twins. At his side, his fluffy white dog, a Great Pyrenees, was always a target for the boys hugs.

One of the twins ran over and jumped in Ben's lap with a toy pistol.

"Daddy, Mommy says we're going to have a little sister."

Startled, Ben looked over at Suellen, who nodded and winked at him.

Life could not be better, Ben thought as he grinned at her.

Time had healed old wounds, but Ben could never forget the reasons a skinny little kid had run away from home in a rain storm. Nor the sight of his tormentor lying in the street, an end to the years of nightmares and regrets.

Every misery, every trail, every struggle had led to this joyous moment. As Suellen laughed with their boys, she cast a sweet smile his way.

He would forever give thanks, and he promised himself his family would always have love, laughter, and wonderment.

ABOUT THE AUTHOR

Western novelist and screenwriter **Lee Martin** grew up on cattle ranches in Northern California. Martin began writing in the third grade and, later in life, wrote and sold 43 short stories before turning to novels with 23 now published. Martin is also a prolific writer of screenplays, mostly Westerns.

Martin's recent novels, *The Grant Conspiracy*, *The Last Wild Ride*, and *Fury at Cross Creek*, all received rave reviews from *True West Magazine* and were based on Martin's screenplays, as is *Fast Ride to Boot Hill. In Mysterious Ways*, Martin's new modern suspense Western, received great critical acclaim from *Kirkus Reviews* and *Midwest Book Reviews*. *Trail of the Fast Gun* is the first book of seven in The Darringer Brothers series, all of which have been reissued in paperback and ebook by Vaca Mountain Press, along with many of Martin's earlier novels.

Martin left the practice of law to write full-time, primarily concentrating on Western screenplays and novels, and often converting one to the other. Martin's screenplay for *Shadow on the Mesa*, starring Kevin Sorbo, Wes Brown, and Gail O'Grady, was based on Martin's novel of the same title (Five

Star Publishing, 2014). The movie was the second-highest-rated and second-most-watched original movie in Hallmark Movie Channel's history when it premiered in 2013. The film also won the prestigious Wrangler Award given by the National Cowboy & Heritage Museum in Oklahoma City for Best Original TV Western Movie. Several of Martin's screenplays are currently under option by producers. *The Siege at Rhyker's Station* and *The Desperate Riders*, based on two of Martin's screenplays, are both being filmed in the Fall of 2020, and will eventually be available as novels. To learn more, visit Lee Martin Westerns on Facebook.

Made in the USA
Middletown, DE
22 October 2023